A SOUTH HILL
CHRISTMAS KEEPSAKE

A South Hill Christmas Keepsake

Nancy Naigle

A SOUTH HILL CHRISTMAS KEEPSAKE
Copyright © 2025, Nancy Naigle
Paperback ISBN: 978-1-948320-08-5
Digital ISBN: 978-1948320078

Release, November 2025

Crossroads Publishing House
P.O. Box 274
Franklin, VA 23851

CHRISTMAS BOOKS by NANCY NAIGLE

Christmas Joy
Hope at Christmas
The Christmas Shop
Christmas Angels
A Heartfelt Christmas Promise
Mission: Merry Christmas
Christmas in Chestnut Ridge

The Secret Ingredient

Chestnut Ridge Novels
And Then There Was You
Christmas in Chestnut Ridge

Shell Collector Novels
The Shell Collector
To Light the Way Forward
Home No Matter Where

…and over 30 more to choose from.

USA TODAY and ECPA Bestselling Author
Nancy Naigle has written over forty novels.

Discover the rest of Nancy's novels at
www.nancynaigle.com
and download your free checklist.

For my friends and neighbors in South Hill—
Your enthusiasm, your spirit, and your steadfast support
have meant more than words can say.
I hope every day feels like Christmas.

CHAPTER ONE

"If Evergreen, Vermont, ever had a rival…South Hill, Virginia, at Christmas might just be it," Hannah Leigh Parker said to herself, "especially with Aunt Winnie hosting the festival." She steered south on I-85 with the car heater on full blast. The road curved through rolling stretches of harvested winter farmland.

Every mile pulled her closer to the town she'd spent the last ten years avoiding, along with the old choices and what-ifs she'd buried right beside it.

Her fingers gripped the wheel. After losing her job and walking away from a relationship built on broken promises, there wasn't much left to hold her in D.C. During Thanksgiving, while others ate with family, she packed her belongings in a storage pod, unsure of where her next job might take her.

Before locking the apartment door for the last time, she'd sent out a handful of résumés. One was to Bank of America in Charlotte. A corporate events position. Her dream job. The one she'd been working toward all along.

She hadn't breathed a word about applying for that one. Not even to Aunt Winnie. Maybe out of fear she'd jinx it after what happened with Evan and her job.

Evan had called their breakup an amicable split, the kind professionals made over lattes and quarterly reports. It was her heartbreak, not his. She could tell by the way his voice stayed calm while hers trembled. He'd already moved on, probably to someone who fit neatly into his calendar.

They'd mixed business and promises, both of which turned out hollow. He'd dangled a future at the huge real estate firm. An offer, as it turned out, that had never really been his to make. She'd planned and delivered the perfect event for them just as she'd promised. But as soon as it was done, so was he. The promotion vanished, the truth unraveled, and the lies came into focus.

The memory still stung as sharp as an icy draft through a cracked window, reminding her she hadn't seen the end coming until it was already over.

Hannah Leigh did not like being played the fool.

Aunt Winnie's phone call had come at the perfect moment. Hannah Leigh jumped at the chance to return to South Hill to help with the big holiday festival. It would be the perfect distraction while she put Evan in the rearview mirror, or better yet, in the dumpster behind it.

She knew Aunt Winnie was hoping this visit might turn into something more permanent, but Hannah Leigh planned to be careful not to feed that hope. This was only a holiday visit, nothing more. Come the new year, she'd be ready to start fresh with a new job, better luck, a clearer vision, and maybe even a little grace for herself.

Three hours and a dozen Christmas songs later, the city lights were a memory in her rearview mirror. The closer she got to South Hill, traffic thinned, the sky cleared, even her heartbeat slowed.

The first twinkling lights of South Hill came into view. This was the perfect place to take a pause before rebooting her career and self-esteem.

Aunt Winnie's lengthy description of this year's festival plans replayed in her mind. It seemed straight out of one of the Hallmark movies Aunt Winnie adored and sounded like it would turn the town into a living snow globe.

Aunt Winnie had taught Hannah Leigh everything she knew about event planning. So, as the Chamber of Commerce's executive director, Winnie was sure to achieve her goal, with or without Hannah Leigh's help.

She had a feeling Aunt Winnie's enthusiasm was spreading faster than cocoa at Bringleton's. By the time she got to South Hill, every strand of twinkle lights within sixty miles would be gone, and every storefront and lamppost would shine like Christmas morning.

With half the town pitching in, she'd be lucky if there was any work left for her to do. Maybe this trip would wind up cocoa, conversation, and a front-row seat to Aunt Winnie's big holiday to-do, and she could act like a tourist for once.

Her body relaxed as she imagined kicking off her shoes and taking a breath without someone dangling deadlines over her head.

There'd been a time when Aunt Winnie's over-the-top Christmas spirit made her cringe.

As a teenager, Hannah Leigh had sworn she'd never recover from the Christmas Aunt Winnie made her wear a red nose and reindeer antlers to the town parade. The photo still resurfaced every December like clockwork. The memory alone was enough to make her cheeks warm all over again.

But after too many late nights and a heartbreak built on broken promises in D.C., Hannah Leigh craved Aunt

Winnie's endless sparkle.

A town that still believes in happiness might be exactly what my weary heart needs. Heck, I might even volunteer to wear those antlers this time.

Her car's Bluetooth dashboard suddenly lit up with a row of emojis. Candy canes, snowflakes, and exclamation points as if Winnie were staging a digital parade. It seemed she was plotting and planning, fussing and finessing directly from Santa's playbook, and expected everyone in town to join the team.

Hannah Leigh turned off Route 58 with a breath of excitement.

The city skyline had long faded in her rearview. Pines gave way to fields now bare following the tobacco harvest, and dusted with white frost, as the "Welcome to South Hill" sign came into view.

She felt sort of bad now. When Aunt Winnie first called, she'd grumbled her way through the promise to help with South Hill's Hometown Holiday Festival. But now, as she caught her first glimpse of downtown, she found herself completely drawn in.

Her heart giddy-upped, and her smile stretched wide as the town unfurled before her with a rush of excitement. Every storefront sparkled with garland and ribbons. Even the law office had a wreath, though the droop suggested it was left from last Christmas.

The taste of Christmas lingered in the air. Sweet, crisp, and with a hint of cinnamon.

It was as if the whole town had dressed up to welcome her home.

Despite her earlier mumbles and second thoughts, a flicker of joy swept through Hannah Leigh. And deep down, she knew this was only the beginning. South Hill still had plenty of Christmas magic waiting to sweep her off her feet.

Lundy Layne Boutique's door stood wide open despite the freezing temperature. Signs boasting holiday dreams on clearance flanked the doors. She was dying to whip into the lot and shop at her favorite boutique, but that would have to wait. Aunt Winnie was expecting her, and she couldn't keep her waiting.

"I'll be back to buy some presents," she said through the window, fluttering her fingertips into a wave to Bria, the store's owner and queen of bringing chic uptown things into this sleepy little town.

And right now, Hannah Leigh had to admit to herself, with a little hope rising inside, that she needed every bit of sparkle South Hill offered.

Thousands of white Christmas lights peppered Main Street, glowing bright as darkness fell over the town. In another week or two, it would be completely dark by this time of day.

Her SUV rattled over a pothole in front of Bringleton's, the coffee shop famous for selling the best dang coffee in the state. The proof was right in front of her. The line stretched out the door, bundled-up customers stamping their boots in the cold, their breath rising in clouds while the sound of laughter spilled out on the street.

Beside it, a hand-painted sign about the 100th anniversary of the Colonial Theater promised holiday movie marathons all year long.

Hannah Leigh shook her head, a smile tugging at her lips. Leave it to South Hill's Chamber of Commerce to turn a Christmas celebration into the shindig of the decade.

"Home sweet holiday circus." She steered her vehicle off the main drag and onto the quieter neighborhood street that led to Aunt Winnie's. Home looked the same, even if she didn't.

CHAPTER TWO

Hannah Leigh's heart beat a nervous two-step as she slowed near Aunt Winnie's house. Things hadn't changed since the last time she'd been here, and it had been a while.

This isn't a permanent arrangement, simply a holiday pit stop, and a chance to breathe.

Still, she knew one thing about coming home. Aunt Winnie would make sure this visit would be memorable.

Sure enough, as Hannah Leigh eased around the big curve to her aunt's street, the familiar white-clapboard house came into view. Pine roping draped the porch in lush loops, every post crowned with a showy red bow.

And there, on the wraparound porch, stood Aunt Winnie herself, waiting as if she'd been tracking Hannah Leigh on Santa's radar. She wore a Christmas sweater lit up like runway lights and balanced a tub the size of a punch bowl in her arms.

A smile broke across Hannah Leigh's face, and the heaviness in her shoulders lifted as she pulled up to the curb.

Oh, Aunt Winnie, you are the show. She climbed out of her car, dusted cookie crumbs from her hoodie, and raced to the porch to wrap her arms around the woman who'd raised her almost as much as her parents.

They hugged until Aunt Winnie pulled back. "Let me take a look at you." Her eyes narrowed. "Just as I suspected. You look skinny." Aunt Winnie juggled the plastic tub against her chest. "But don't worry, I've got cookies, cocoa, and good southern cooking on tap!"

Of course, she did.

"Please tell me that tub you're cradling isn't full of cocoa." Hannah Leigh reached hesitantly. "I remember you telling me Bringleton's is now serving it in quart-sized deli containers."

Aunt Winnie glanced down and smirked, tucking the container under her arm. "No, it is *not*. The cocoa is inside. This," she said, giving the tub a little shake, "is full of teensy styrofoam glitter stars. I'm decorating the porch. Every sparkle counts. You can help me later."

"Here we go," Hannah Leigh said in the sing-song way she and Aunt Winnie had always done when they were teasing.

Aunt Winnie's eyes crinkled, and a soft laugh bubbled up, touched with the comfort of old memories.

She eyed her aunt more closely, blinking back a surge of emotion. "I'm sorry it's been so long since my last visit."

"Don't apologize. I know you miss your folks. It must be hard to come back."

She swallowed back the threat of tears.

"Time flies. Give me a hug." Aunt Winnie set down the tub and flipped her cuffed fingers in her direction. "Bring it in here, kiddo."

Hannah Leigh stepped into another welcoming embrace. *Home.* Aunt Winnie's house was always welcoming.

"And you look like you've been living on caffeine and broken dreams," said Aunt Winnie. "Come on inside. We've got decorating to do, and the mayor's already in a mood."

"Isn't he always in a mood?"

"Now you be nice." Aunt Winnie wagged a finger, but

the twinkle in her eyes told Hannah Leigh that her aunt didn't disagree.

Hannah Leigh didn't so much walk into her aunt's house as get swept up in it. The pine-scented air, a glitter trail across the floor, and a towering Fraser fir whose angel nearly scraped the ceiling were no surprise; this was Aunt Winnie's Christmas trifecta.

"This year's gonna be something special," Winnie said, eyes sparkling as she thrust a string of lights into Hannah Leigh's hands. "The first annual South Hill Hometown Holiday Festival isn't only a week of events. It's going to be the whole heartbeat of Christmas around here from now on."

Her aunt's enthusiasm tickled her. "I can see it," Hannah Leigh teased, raising her arms like a movie director framing a shot. "Lights brighter than Broadway. Cocoa served with mounds of marshmallows. And the finale? Enough sparkle to make an elf blush."

"You think you're funny? Girl, this is serious business." She wagged a finger in Hannah Leigh's direction. "Mark my words, you're going to thank your lucky stars you didn't miss it. We're even bringing back the Minnie Pearl Pralines," Aunt Winnie said proudly.

"I guess I'd better make $1.98 price tags on strings to hang from them, like on her hat in her Hee-Haw heyday."

"I was shooting for two bucks, but you're right. The $1.98 is the perfect call bag. You know, that price-tag schtick started right here in our town. Not on that show. Back then, she performed at the Colonial Theater," Aunt Winnie said, her eyes lighting with pride.

"Really?"

"I wouldn't lie about a thing like that. It was never a gimmick, just a lucky accident. You see, Johnny Ray, the prop fella, forgot to take the tag off Minnie's hat before she went onstage. In the middle of her performance, the tag swung right down in front of her nose, but Minnie didn't miss a beat. She simply tipped her head, cracked a joke, and started singing. The crowd roared, and from that point on, that tag became her trademark."

"Didn't she fall in love with the high school principal while she was in town? Or was that a rumor?"

"Not a rumor at all," Aunt Winnie said, eyes twinkling. "She made him her special pralines, and he couldn't get enough of them, or her. They were the talk of the town back then. He was a teacher, older and respectable, supposed to be setting an example, and there he was keeping company with a young up-and-coming performer." She gave a knowing shake of her head. "This was before her big break, of course, but still…a young actress and a schoolteacher? In the sixties? Mercy, folks didn't know whether to clutch their pearls or polish them. But that's another story."

"Be careful tarnishing an American icon's image, Auntie," Hannah Leigh teased.

"They were in love. Nothing wrong with that. And guess what, this isn't your average praline recipe. I got it straight from her niece's church cookbook. We're doing a pop-up booth to sell them during the tree lighting. You'll help, of course."

"Of course," Hannah Leigh echoed again.

For the next hour, they fluffed garlands while Hannah Leigh untangled her thoughts as much as the lights. Thank goodness she'd stay busy enough not to spend too much time thinking about all the time she wasted on you-know-who. Considering that made her queasy.

Outside, Aunt Winnie fussed over things. "Come on out

here, Hannah Leigh."

She walked outside.

At the foot of the steps stood Aunt Winnie, holding an extension cord. "Get down here."

She hurried to join her aunt. "I'm ready."

Aunt Winnie's face brightened like a crazy scientist when she connected the wires.

The whole place turned into a winter-like wonderland, even though some Christmases they never got real snow, just the kind that's pretty to look at, and gone the next day before you have to drive to work. South Hill might not have Vermont's icicles, but it had heart.

Hannah Leigh scanned everything, trying to take it all in. "How did you—"

Aunt Winnie squeezed Hannah Leigh into a side hug. "Honey, I've been working on it for weeks."

"Wow." If Aunt Winnie had her way, there'd be enough light displays to rival Times Square and make everyone forget about snow, or the lack thereof.

"Oh, honey, this is just the warm up," said Aunt Winnie. "Wait until you see them all lit at once! Help me plug them in."

It took a few minutes, and a lot of extension cords, but Hannah Leigh was pretty sure astronauts on the International Space Station needed sunglasses tonight.

"Rudolph is going to need sunglasses," Hannah Leigh joked. "It's perfect."

"Yes, it is." Her aunt gave it an approving nod. "Now, let's make the rest of the town get the holiday spirit, too.

CHAPTER THREE

Aunt Winnie pressed a clipboard and a homemade oatmeal raisin cookie into Hannah Leigh's hands before she could even catch a breath.

The list of to-dos was long. The judging criteria for the gingerbread contest stretched a mile and twice as detailed.

Evan would've required the plan to be color-coded, printed on heavy cardstock, and emailed as a digital backup. Aunt Winnie preferred the clipboard-and-cookie approach. Hannah Leigh found she didn't mind the trade. *Good riddance, Evan.*

"No more stalling," Winnie declared, tucking a pen behind her ear. "The gingerbread nativity contest won't judge itself, and you promised to be my right hand."

So much for easing into Christmas. Apparently, rest wasn't on the schedule until after New Year's.

Winnie moved briskly through the house, her shoes tapping in quick, decisive steps as she led the way.

"Stalling? I haven't even been here long enough to stall." Hannah Leigh scanned her clipboard of tasks. "Is the gingerbread nativity contest tonight?"

"The judging is tonight. We will award the winner's ribbons before the display is open to the public. Let's go."

Hannah Leigh opened her mouth to protest, but Winnie handed her a travel mug of cocoa and directed her firmly into the car, reminding her to smile as if she were on the

Chamber payroll.

"Wait until you see Dogwood Hall in person," Aunt Winnie said as she got into the car. "The pictures I sent don't do it justice."

The ride was quick, and shoppers filled Main Street. When they pulled into the venue parking lot, the parking lot was full, and the sky was full of stars.

The long, low brick school had sat empty since her teens, when a new campus opened across town. Once a squat brown school with tired blue panels, the building now looked fresh in glossy white, board-and-batten siding giving it a modern farmhouse charm. The windows shone with promise.

For generations, the old auditorium served as the place that fed them at noon and tested their jump shots by night. Part cafeteria, part gym, it was where the whole town had gathered for meetings and celebrations.

But now, the chandeliers replaced fluorescent lights, and a fresh, glossy white finish now covered the brick. It was far from a utilitarian building now. It wore the new role of venue well. Pine roping dotted with glossy red ornaments and shiny silver stars hung across its wide double doors, dressing the building for the upcoming holiday.

Winnie tipped her head toward the schoolhouse. "It's hard to believe this old place is hosting the opening night of the South Hill Hometown Holiday Festival next week. Dogwood Hall. Ain't she grand? If this doesn't bring the past and present together, I don't know what will."

Hannah Leigh stared at it from the sidewalk, breath catching in her chest.

Aunt Winnie snapped her fingers. "Don't dally. Gingerbread awaits."

They slipped in through the back. Muffled carols and the peppery scent of freshly baked gingerbread washed over Hannah Leigh, making her hungry. Tables stretched wall to wall. Each displayed a gingerbread creation more ambitious—*and some more lopsided, bless their hearts*—than the last. Some actually even looked like a nativity scene.

Winnie handed Hannah Leigh a clipboard and pointed toward the first entry, where the stable roof sagged under a snowdrift of powdered sugar. "Structural integrity: questionable. Spirit of Christmas: excellent."

Hannah Leigh's smile tilted, the mischief clear in her tone. "Well, bless them, at least these sheep don't look like they wandered out of s'mores accident." She gestured toward the gingerbread beside it. "That's a win."

They moved to the next table where the wise men leaned precariously, one gumdrop crown sliding down his frosted forehead.

Winnie adjusted her glasses, made a sharp note on her clipboard, and muttered, "Deduct for decapitation risk. Can't have headless gingerbread in South Hill."

At the third table, Hannah Leigh leaned closer. "Are those graham cracker crowns on the wise men?"

Aunt Winnie gave a measured nod. "Looks like those wise men stopped by the bake sale on their way."

"And is that orange gumdrop on a toothpick supposed to be gold, frankincense, or myrrh?"

Aunt Winnie smiled. "Honey, around here it's more likely barbecue sauce." She snorted into her cocoa, trying to compose herself. "Points for originality," she said as she scribbled her pen across the scorecard.

They covered the entire area, their scorecards full of

notes, stars, smiley faces, and more exclamation points than numbers.

Aunt Winnie tapped her pen against the clipboard. "Numbers are fine for accountants," she said, "but I've been judging these contests since folks used saltines for shingles. Sometimes a smiley face says it better."

Her system wasn't fancy, but everyone in South Hill trusted it. Over the years, her stars, hearts, and exclamation points had become their own kind of language—one only Aunt Winnie could truly translate.

Aunt Winnie tapped her pen against her chin. "All right, tally time. You add, I'll sip."

Hannah Leigh squinted at the score sheet. "You gave someone a ten and a frowny face."

"That was for structural integrity," Winnie said in a serious tone. "The roof caved, but the spirit stood strong."

"Uh-huh." Hannah Leigh pretended to add up the numbers, then looked up. "So we agreed, the peppermint stick roof with the wise men takes first?"

Winnie sighed dramatically. "Fine. But only because I can't in good conscience give second place to a stable made entirely of pretzel sticks."

"Deal," Hannah Leigh said, grinning as she circled the winner's name.

"Well," Winnie huffed, shoving the results into her folder, "South Hill's future architects may be working with frosting instead of blueprints, but they've got heart. I'll get the certificates done tonight, and we'll position the ribbons tomorrow."

"Nobody does Christmas quite like South Hill."

"You can take that to the bank." Aunt Winnie dug in her pocket for her keys and headed for the front entrance door.

"Come on. You've got to see the dogwood."

Hannah Leigh fell in step behind her, quick stepping to keep up.

Aunt Winnie called over her shoulder. "Did I tell you our dogwood is now the oldest one in *all* of Virginia?"

"No. We've been the second oldest for as long as I can remember. How'd that happen?" Hannah Leigh had this precarious image of Aunt Winnie with eye black smudged on her face, belly-crawling her way in the darkness to take out the number one dogwood to get the bragging rights. "Please tell me it was a natural death."

"Lightning, actually." Aunt Winnie pushed open the heavy doors to the front lawn, where the dogwood proudly stood in front of the former South Hill K–12 schoolhouse. "You've got to see this."

CHAPTER FOUR

Hannah Leigh remembered being a kid and slipping beneath those limbs at recess with a Nancy Drew paperback while other children chased each other across the playground. The gentle rustle of leaves overhead whispered promises, like secrets only time could unlock.

The arching branches stretched out, as if holding old memories and hopes.

"I love this tree." Hannah Leigh wondered how many others held thoughtful memories of this old tree in their hearts.

"Do you remember the legend?" Aunt Winnie's expression softened.

"I remember it was called the Lost Love Tree, but I never knew why." Hannah Leigh studied the dogwood, her eyes tracing the rough, intricate pattern of its weathered bark. Its limbs twisted in silent choreography in the winter breeze, bending as if to guard and protect all the memories.

"Mmm-hmm," Winnie said, her breath clouding in the cold. "Back when this was still the town school, a young teacher and a traveling newspaperman fell in love while he was here on assignment. Henry was doing a story on the railroad expansion, but he had to leave for another assignment when he was done. He asked her to meet him at the dogwood on Christmas Eve."

Aunt Winnie continued, "People say that the man was so smitten, he planned to propose before catching the midnight train and taking her with him."

Hannah Leigh could picture the young newspaperman standing in a halo of lantern light, flakes tumbling through the glow and clinging to the dogwood's limbs as he waited to ask the girl of his dreams to marry him. "That is so romantic. So, they got engaged right here?"

"No, they didn't. A terrible snowstorm rolled in, making the roads nearly impassable and threatening a foot of powder. They say he waited here by this tree until the last train came through, but his love never showed. He had to be on the last train out that night for a new assignment, and the way the story goes, they never saw each other again."

"That's heartbreaking."

Aunt Winnie's lips pursed. "People say they left letters wedged between the limbs of this tree the whole time he was in town. Decades later, someone found an old love letter that Henry must've left that night of the storm. That's how we know his intentions. That's when folks started calling it the Lost Love Tree."

"Where's that letter now?"

Aunt Winnie cocked her head. "I'm not entirely sure. We should have it on display somewhere. As the story goes, the woman grieved his leaving so deeply that she took to her bed, and some say she left to look for him and never came back."

"She must be really old. Could she still be alive?"

Winnie's eyes flew wide. "Mind your mouth, young lady. Old is a state of mind, I'll have you know."

"Oh, stop! You're not old." Aunt Winnie might never be old, despite her years. Hannah Leigh's heart fluttered. "Can you imagine if they'd gotten engaged here, or even married beneath the dogwood while it's in full bloom?"

"Yes. I can." Aunt Winnie's features softened. "It would be beautiful. No one has ever married under this tree that I've heard about. This tree might be waiting for a love story to keep the appointment."

"Perhaps that's why it's lived so long," Hannah Leigh said.

"Guess we'll never know." Aunt Winnie smiled, then glanced at her watch. With a quick hug, she tugged on Hannah Leigh's sleeve. "Oh dear, I need to check something at the office. Let's walk. It's not far."

"Sure." She didn't mind a Southern winter kind of cold, the sort that shows your breath without chasing you indoors. It was nice to take a stroll with no agenda and no phone ringing in her ear.

As they neared the Chamber of Commerce, South Hill's iconic LOVE sign came into view, standing proudly out front. They created it entirely from old railway parts. A rusted RR Crossing sign for the "L," a spoked train wheel for the "O," a pair of antique track tongs for the "V," and reclaimed railroad ties forming the "E." The sight made her smile. It had been the backdrop for her high-school graduation photos, back when she couldn't wait to leave town.

As they passed, a young couple snuggled up close for a selfie, laughing as their golden retriever leapt into the frame at the last second, ears flying and tail wagging like he'd planned the photobomb all along.

Hannah Leigh's heart danced, caught between envy and nostalgia as she watched the couple. "What's next on the list?"

"Tomorrow, you're helping Nate Collier set up wreaths and garland at the old school. He's turning the gym into a winter wonderland for the festival."

"Nate?" Hannah Leigh echoed, the name tugging at something old and unresolved. "As in... Nate Collier from school?"

"Don't worry. He got taller. And kinder." Aunt Winnie's eyes twinkled. "Mostly. I mean, sometimes he can show a little temper if there's a bad call on the field. Did I mention he coaches football on the side?"

"You didn't, but he was an outstanding player in high school. If he coaches on the side, what does he do for a job?"

"He's a contractor. A good one, too. He is a real craftsman, not one of those who take shortcuts. He's well respected around here."

Her palms began to sweat. Nate Collier. She hadn't said that name out loud in years, but it still carried a spark of what-if she didn't trust anymore. Not after Evan. The idea of seeing Nate again made her pulse quicken in equal parts curiosity and dread. She wasn't ready for anyone's charm, least of all the boy she'd once written his name in the margins of her notebook beside hers.

Before Hannah Leigh could protest, a big gust of wind caught her off balance, tugging at the clipboard Aunt Winnie had assigned to her like it had something personal against her holiday plans. She pinned it against her chest, sighed, and squinted up at the banner above the sidewalk that was hanging slightly crooked.

Tree Lighting Ceremony
Friday, December 12, 7 PM

From down the block, a sputtering, puttering motor grew louder.

"Oh no," Hannah Leigh muttered under her breath. "Is that Birdie?"

"She hasn't changed a bit," Aunt Winnie said. "Well, she might be even more audacious."

Sure enough, here came Birdie, swaddled in tartan plaid and driving her bedazzled baby-blue golf cart like it was a presidential motorcade. A wreath the size of a Smart car was zip-tied to the front, glittering like a disco ball in the midday sun. "Jingle Bell Rock" blared from a speaker strapped to the back.

"Heads up, sugarplum! I'm comin' in hot!" she squealed, red hair flying.

Hannah Leigh stepped aside just in time for *The Gossip*, Birdie's appropriately named golf cart, to roll to a bouncy stop against the curb.

Birdie flung herself out of the doorless side as if she were exiting a limousine. Birdie's red sweater had a reindeer with a light-up nose, and she wore a matching lipstick shade, possibly named *Cranberry Chaos*.

"I was just at Harper's Jewelry, and I have *news*. You remember that ring they kept in the display case for years, the one with the two little dogwood blossoms on either side of the diamond? Gone. Sold this morning. And not to whom you'd guess."

Aunt Winnie's eyes widened. "Not Billy for Sonja?"

Birdie's lips curled, not totally unlike the Grinch. "Nope. An out of towner. I can't believe they sold it to someone with no connection to our tree! What were they thinking?"

"That a sale is a sale?" Seemed perfectly acceptable to Hannah Leigh.

"Don't be silly, child!" Aunt Winnie nearly shuddered. "Remind me to give you my bracelet to take over there to get fixed. The darn thing flew off my wrist right in the middle of choir practice last week. Nearly clocked poor Pastor Qualls right in the halo."

"Oh, goodness gracious. We can't have that! I'll get the bracelet over there," Hannah Leigh said, then turned to Birdie. "How have you been?"

Birdie cast her a disappointed look. "Oh, I'm swell. Arthritis is barkin' and I sat on a caramel earlier, but otherwise, I'm upright. About time you came back."

"Thanks for the warm welcome," Hannah Leigh said, regretting the passive-aggressive tone. "I'm just here to help with the festival."

"Oh goodness. Well, your aunt has her work cut out this year. Don't get me started on the mayor and his opinion of Christmas lights. Patsy Blackwood, who's *twice* removed from city business but still knows everything, said the mayor vetoed red-and-green bulbs on the stoplights because they looked 'too playful.' I'm sure he'll be by soon to remind everyone that Christmas cheer requires a permit."

"I'm ready for him," Aunt Winnie said.

Birdie leaned in and stage-whispered, "That man has the personality of last year's Christmas tree. Dry, prickly, and shedding needles where nobody wants 'em.'"

Hannah Leigh stifled a laugh.

"I figured I'd drop by, lend a hand, offer unsolicited commentary, and refill my cocoa tub." Birdie's energy was boundless. "Lord knows those girls in the coffee shop give me the 'ma'am limit' after noon."

She dropped into a folding chair beside the supply bins, pulled out a mint from her purse, and began humming.

And just like that, *Birdie Horn was officially on site.*

"Did anyone tell you we're bringing back Minnie Pearl's Pralines?" Birdie said before either woman could speak. "And mercy, they finally fixed the lights on the Colonial marquee. Took a hundred years and a box of spare bulbs, but hallelujah, she's glowing again like the good old days."

"That's a long time, but the theater looks better than I remember."

"Which, by the way," Birdie said, "is about as long as it seems since I've seen you around here. About time you came back. Good timing, too. We're stirring up a blizzard of Christmas cheer around here."

As Birdie bustled off, Hannah Leigh lingered on the sidewalk a moment longer. The LOVE sign stirred a rush of memories. It surprised her Aunt Winnie hadn't already dressed it in garland and lights. She might slip back afterward and do a little magic on the sign after Aunt Winnie goes to sleep to surprise her.

Looking down the block, she watched Main Street brighten as each shop window lit up with its own unique style, the combined lights stitching the pavement into a holiday quilt.

At long last, a gentle certainty settled in her chest. She belonged here. It felt as if the town itself was wrapping her in a warm welcome and quietly saving a few surprises just for her.

CHAPTER FIVE

If you wanted to find the heart of South Hill on any morning, Nate Collier knew you started at Bringleton's, where the coffee came in thirty-two-ounce buckets big enough to warm your soul and half your extended family. And if he timed it right, like he did today, he could swing by The Doughnut Den first for a cinnamon twist the size of a flashlight, perfect for dunking.

The bag dangled from his hand as he walked down Main Street, impressed by all the changes that seemed to have happened overnight. Wreaths crowned lampposts to Graham Hardware, garland linked storefronts, and if he knew Birdie Horn, those candy-cane zip ties on the trash cans had her fingerprints all over them.

He rarely got to Bringleton's this early, but the day had started with an itch he couldn't name. It was the kind that made a man reach for caffeine and an empty seat by a window simply to think, and this was the place.

Cinnamon from the paper bag wafted into the air as he pushed the glass door open. The familiar jingle welcomed him like an old friend.

Nodding to the regulars already lined up along the counter, he waited for his turn to order his coffee.

He claimed his usual seat by the window and pulled the cinnamon roll from the pastry bag. One generous bite, a long sip of coffee, and the world slowed enough for him to scroll through his phone for the project updates from his crew. The old Safeway conversion was ahead of schedule; the Town Hall remodel, thanks to the mayor's ever-shifting list of "must-haves," was another story.

The bell jingled again, capturing his attention, but he didn't even have to look up to recognize the familiar shuffle of his uncle's boots.

Speak of the devil.

Mayor Clarence Collier, his uncle, grumbled a good morning to the barista and ordered a double shot of espresso. Black, no fuss.

"Morning, Nate." Clarence took the espresso, making himself at home in the chair across from him.

"Have a seat." It was a smart-aleck response, but Uncle Clarence had a way of inserting himself. "Didn't expect to see you in here before eight," Nate said, offering a half-smile.

"I had insider information that the first praline batch was coming out of the oven this morning." He glanced at his watch, tapping its face, "…right about now. Figured I'd snag a couple before Birdie cleared the entire tray."

Nate huffed a laugh. "Smart man."

They lapsed into silence, the kind that settled between folks who didn't need to fill every second with words. Nate took a sip of his coffee and glanced out the window. An SUV eased to the curb, and he'd recognize the silhouette of the driver anywhere.

Hannah Leigh Parker? Lord have mercy.

She stepped out, all bundled up in a cranberry red coat,

scarf loose around her neck, her cheeks pink from the cold. She waved to someone across the street and ducked into the jewelry store.

Something outside drew Clarence's eye, his expression shifting. "Would you look there? That's—"

"Hannah Leigh," Nate finished. She hadn't changed much. That same easy, sunlit smile, but she carried herself differently, more sure, more herself. He remembered the way she used to tuck straight hair behind her ear when she got nervous—always tidy, always in control. Now it fell longer and freer, loose curls past her shoulders like she'd allowed herself to let loose a little. The light caught on those chestnut strands, and for a second, it hit him how much growing up they'd both done.

Clarence raised one brow. "Well, I'll be."

Nate didn't answer. He didn't need to. The mayor was quite aware of Nate's high school crush on that girl. The whole town probably remembered it, even though it had been so many years ago. "Yeah, it's been a minute since she's been around here."

"She has that big job up in D.C.. I heard her aunt roped her into helping with the Chamber of Commerce Christmas festivities this year," Clarence added. "She's back for the holidays."

Nate sipped his coffee, hiding the sudden jolt.

Clarence took a sip of his espresso and leaned in, lowering his voice. "With the Hometown Holiday Festival kicking off, we'll need every garland and wreath we can find. Winnie has already asked that I volunteer you to help with setup. Of course, I told her you'd be happy to do it."

His uncle was always quick to volunteer him. It would be nice if he'd at least once asked. "Let me guess. Hannah Leigh's helping with the decorating, too?"

"Didn't ask, but I'd guess yes." Clarence nodded. "Might as well make peace with the idea. You'll be seeing a lot of her over the holiday."

Nate blew out a breath. "It's fine. We were friends once. I can handle it."

Clarence gave him a look that said he wasn't buying it, but he didn't push.

The silence pushed Nate to his feet. He clapped his uncle on the shoulder and headed out into the crisp air.

Crossing Atlantic Street to the next block, the town's LOVE sign shone in the morning sun. Someone had wrapped candy cane-striped ribbon around it overnight.

He smiled at the sight. That's what he loved about this town. It never waited for perfection. It just showed up with what it had and made it beautiful.

As he rounded the corner toward the schoolhouse project site, his phone buzzed.

WINNIE: Need you to swing by the Dogwood Hall by 10.
WINNIE: Hannah Leigh will meet you. Be nice. Don't scare her off.

He rolled his eyes, typing back.

NATE: I'm always nice. You're thinking of Uncle Clarence.

Why was everyone acting like it was such a big deal for him to see Hannah Leigh? Their history, well, it was just that…history. They had been kids.

Winnie texted back the emoji with the winking face and tongue stuck out.

"What? Winnie. You did not just send that." But he didn't respond. Letting it go was the mature way to handle that. He didn't mind helping Hannah Leigh. Not really. It might be nice to have the chance to get to meet the grown-up version of the girl who once made his teenage heart trip over itself like a Christmas puppy on polished floors.

Perhaps Christmas this year would center on more than just decorations. Maybe, just maybe, it was about a second chance.

He walked over to the school. Looking out over the now landscaped area that used to be the playground, he remembered chasing Hannah Leigh Parker around the monkey bars. He wasn't sure what he'd have done if he'd ever caught her, but there was excitement and giggles in the effort, and that had been enough.

He checked his watch for the third time, but still didn't move toward the door. Showing up early would scream eager, and he wasn't about to give the whole town, or Hannah Leigh, that kind of headline. The gossip grapevine would love that.

So, he tightened the bow on the wreath of the front entrance and then lingered over his coffee like he had nothing better to do, dragging out every minute until the clock finally caught up with him.

At exactly ten o'clock, he climbed the old schoolhouse steps. The venue smelled of wood polish and holiday spice. This building had been everything from a haunted house to a voting precinct since the school closed. Today, it was hard to recognize this place.

Nate's boots sounded heavy against the floors as he walked to the new community event space. His team had done the heavy lifting on this renovation.

Inside, the high ceilings still held the original tin tiles, and the windows, now re-glazed and painted a soft antique cream, caught the morning light perfectly. He took it in. There was something about restoring the bones of an old building that settled the ache in his chest like nothing else.

He'd been working on this project on and off all fall, ever since his uncle, the mayor, had reluctantly agreed to move the opening of the venue up for this year's Christmas events. Nate didn't ask questions about the change of heart. He simply picked up his hammer and said, "Yes."

Today, though, he wasn't alone. Which was a wrinkle.

The minute he'd seen Hannah Leigh in front of Bringleton's that morning, dressed in boots, a cable-knit sweater, and looking every bit like she belonged in one of those fancy Christmas catalogs, you could've knocked Nate over with a candy cane. She hadn't changed. Not in how it mattered. Still pretty, still had that same spark in her blue eyes that made him feel like he was standing in the path of something important.

For the first time in a long while, Nate didn't mind the waiting.

CHAPTER SIX

Nate tried to look nonchalant as Hannah Leigh stepped into his path, carrying a big plastic tub and placing it next to a stack of others just like it.

"I figured you'd be halfway through the lights by now." The bin rustled with every step.

Nate blurted out a little white lie, "I got delayed making sure Birdie didn't glue tinsel to the exit signs. Again."

"Sounds like her." Hannah Leigh shook her head. The familiar warmth cracked the cold bite in the air. "She means well."

"So do fireworks, but they're still loud, messy, and best admired from a safe distance."

She walked past him, brushing a strand of hair behind her ear, and set the bin down with a thump. "I heard you worked on the remodel of this place. I'd never have known this used to be a school."

His shoulders lifted a bit. "Thanks. It's been a labor of love. It'll be cool to see how the town uses Dogwood Hall for the holidays. You know how the town gets when Christmas rolls around."

Hannah Leigh tilted her head, a teasing glint in her eye. "Like a sugar rush with a to-do list?"

He gave a low, good-natured laugh. "Exactly."

"Only Aunt Winnie seems determined to outdo her best this year."

Nate rubbed the back of his neck. "Not a simple task," he said, knowing that also meant his job would be bigger too. "So, I hear we're putting up lights."

"Yep." She raised a tangled ball of lights from the top of the box she'd brought in. "Santa's spaghetti, anyone? It'll take longer to untangle this mess than to hang them."

He eyed the mess. "Well, with both of us working on it, I'm sure we can get it done."

They got to work in companionable silence, untangling strings of lights to hang, the kind that blinked with the rhythm of a country fiddle. As they worked, Hannah Leigh ran her fingers across the edge of the windowsill, pausing.

"This used to be my classroom in the fourth grade. Miss Parrish. She had a thing for cardinal decorations."

"I remember that about her," Nate said. "She moved away a few years ago."

"Aunt Winnie received a postcard from her last year from Florida where her daughter lives. Said she misses the dogwood blooms but not the snow."

"Can't say I'd blame her." He held up a length of flocked garland. "This should fit right over that doorway. What do you think?"

"It'll be perfect." She took the other end, and they walked over to install it.

Nate hammered a few nails into the wall so they could drape it around the door frame. His arm brushed against Hannah Leigh as she lifted the garland up to him.

He froze, and she didn't budge. He tried to subdue the zing that had shot through him, cleared his throat, and changed the subject. "How have things been going?"

She glanced at him. "Pretty good. I thought coming back here would be hard, but it's been nice so far."

"Yeah. I get that. You're used to being in the city. This probably isn't that exciting to you."

"No. Not at all." She looked across the space. "It's nice to see so many familiar faces all pitching in." She lifted an untangled string of lights for him to hang.

He made quick work of it. He wanted to say more. To ask about the job in D.C. and the reason behind that shadow in her eyes. Instead, he picked up the extension cord and plugged in the lights.

They both turned to admire the colorful glow over the doorway of Dogwood Hall.

"It's beautiful," she said.

"Needs people, music, and hot cocoa in a cup the size of a mop bucket."

"Of course." Her hands came together, curling as though around a mug of something warm. "Bringleton's. It was always the best."

"Still is. You know what…hold that thought. I'll be right back." He dashed out to his truck. Her laugh stayed with him all the way back to his truck, soft as sawdust and twice as impossible to shake.

For a half-second, he considered driving to Bringleton's, but with it only a quarter mile away, he'd probably spend more time parking, so he broke into a jog toward the coffee shop.

It didn't take long to grab what he'd gone for. When he stepped back inside, the warmth of the room hit him, and so did the dorkiness creeping up on him for how much effort he'd just spent on cocoa.

Hannah Leigh glanced up from the garland she was untangling, a puzzled smile on her face. "Where did you run off to?"

Nate lifted the box in his hands. Two massive thirty-two-ounce tubs of hot cocoa sloshed inside. "Emergency supply run. Figured we'd earn it before the day's through."

He handed her one.

"This is crazy. It's the size you'd get enough potato salad for the whole family." Steam curled from holes punched in the lids. "Smells good though." She sipped, closing her eyes as the sweetness hit her. "Is this much hot cocoa in one sitting even legal?"

"This is South Hill. We measure caffeine and sugar by the quart these days." He shrugged. "Let's sit outside. It's nice."

She followed him outside to enjoy the mid-morning sun washing over the town. "Thanks for the cocoa and your help."

He admitted they hadn't given him a choice. "I don't mind."

"Me neither." Her smile came easily, but silence fell between them as they sat on the bench. "I swear I might overdose on this much chocolate."

He nodded. "The whole town might become diabetic if this trend lasts past the holidays," he admitted.

"The mayor might have to create a new violation for that."

"Don't tempt him," Nate warned.

She leaned forward, resting her forearms on her knees. "I

forgot how quiet it is here. You can hear yourself think. It's nice." She seemed to catch herself. "For a visit."

Nate smiled, tucking his hands into his jacket pockets. "Careful. This town reels folks in before they know what hit 'em."

She glanced over, one brow lifting. "How's that?"

"Starts with a visit," he said, eyes on the horizon. "Next thing you know, you don't want to leave."

"This hasn't been home for a long time." Hannah Leigh looked away, a teasing smile tugging at her lips. "Don't worry. I'm just passing through, not settling in."

"Guess we'll see." He couldn't resist. "Who knows, maybe now you're where you're supposed to be."

She didn't answer, but her doubtful expression told him everything he needed to know.

"I have an idea," he said. "How about we do something spontaneous? Something that didn't make the clipboard?"

Her mouth opened, and he braced himself for rejection. "I'm not afraid to do something on a whim. Besides, everything on this morning's list is complete. What's on your mind?"

"Roll up your sleeves, Hannah Leigh, because we are going to make our own rules."

The color drained from her face, but she recovered quickly. "Fine. Let's do this."

He'd thought he'd finished that chapter with Hannah Leigh, but perhaps it wasn't over after all.

CHAPTER SEVEN

By the dogwood, Hannah Leigh's sweater snagged on a long strand of pine roping on the handrail, causing her to nearly trip over a box of Christmas lights that looked like they'd wrestled with a squirrel and lost. "Lordy goodness." She stumbled, arms windmilling to stay upright. She placed one hand against the tree trunk.

Nate was on the ladder above her, stringing a net of white lights through the twisted limbs of the old dogwood tree that sat like a forgotten relic between the schoolhouse and the sidewalk. "You okay down there?" he asked, glancing over his shoulder with a grin.

"Just trying not to end up a casualty." She tugged at her sweater to free herself. She glanced up at him. He still had that steady, sure look about him—dark hair a little longer now, a day's scruff softening his jaw and making him look more like the man he'd become than the boy she once knew. She played off the mishap. "You'd think after all these years, this tree would've learned not to fight back."

He smirked. "It's got roots deeper than the mayor's grudge against public Wi-Fi. Be gentle. Plus, this tree has never had lights on it."

"Never?"

"Never. The historical society has never allowed it," he said.

"Wait? Are we going to get into trouble for doing this?" The last thing she needed was to get into trouble and smear Winnie's outstanding reputation in this town.

"I told you we were making our own rules. Besides, we'll be fine as long as no one rats us out." He shook his head. "It's an old rule. Don't sweat it. This tree has lived so long, I doubt a few low-voltage lights will cause a problem. Besides, I'm being very gentle."

"You better be!" She shook her head. "We've been out here working for hours. We'd better hurry before we get caught."

"It'll be fine. Trust me." Nate paused, one hand gripping the ladder. "This tree deserves to be celebrated."

Hannah Leigh glanced up, surprised by the wistfulness in his voice. "I bet this tree has seen a lot over the years."

Only the soft rustle of fallen leaves interrupted the silence between them.

The old dogwood, bare of its summer blooms, still carried a quiet dignity. Its branches reached wide across the lawn.

"I used to believe this tree was magic," she said aloud.

Nate looked down from the ladder, his dark brown eyes softened. "Maybe it still is."

She was about to reply when her boot caught on something uneven. Bending down, she brushed aside what she thought was a rock, but her fingers grazed something smooth and curved, half-buried in the soil.

"What in the world..." she murmured, digging until a small pouch came free. Heavy for its size, something solid was tucked inside. Sliding a finger through the drawstring, she loosened it just enough to peek. A small object slipped out, tumbling into the dirt at her feet.

Tarnished with age, a locket lay before her, its chain broken and rusted in two. She eased a fingernail into the edge of the clasp until it gave, revealing two faded black and white photographs that had to be more than fifty years old. One picture of a young woman with soft curls and the other of a man in a suit, both smiling the way people do when they still believe love can fix anything.

"Nate? Come and look at this," she called, brushing dirt off the locket.

He climbed down, wiping his hands on his jeans. "What did you find? That old time capsule from the third grade? Is this where we buried that thing?"

"No, we buried the time capsule out back on the far side of the school playground but look what I found. This has to be even older than that time capsule." She opened the locket and handed it to him. "Do these faces look familiar to you?"

He squinted. "Not really. It could be anybody. Folks used to bury things all the time around here. You wouldn't believe what people find under the garden beds. Someone found a jar of money in a flower bed over on Franklin Street."

"Isn't that where the UFO sighting was back in the 70s? Maybe aliens left a deposit to come back."

"Hope I'm here when they do."

"Not me, but still, this locket..." Hannah Leigh turned it over in her palm. "Look, there are initials etched on the back. *I found my love under the dogwood. RD + HB,* and the date December 23, 1964."

"The eve before Christmas Eve? Over sixty years ago?" Nate let out a low whistle. He studied the locket. "Looks like it's been in the dirt a long time."

"I wonder how it got here?" She turned it over in her palm. "Maybe it was a Christmas gift, and the chain broke while she was sitting under the tree reading, but she didn't realize it."

"Doubtful." He pointed to the slip of fabric. "You don't wrap up something like that by accident."

"Then it had to be a token of true love." She pressed it to her heart. "So sweet."

"Or, it might not have been sweet at all," he said with a twinkle in his eye, "maybe somebody pitched it mid-argument right into a snow drift for dramatic effect." He mimed a pitcher's windup, complete with sound effects and an exaggerated 'boom' at the end.

Her eyes narrowed. "You know how to ruin a perfectly romantic theory."

"Just keeping us grounded in reality."

"Well, reality's overrated." She slipped the locket into her coat pocket. "I'm choosing the love story."

He winced. "Sorry, but that tree's probably seen a lot of breakups over the years."

"Well, according to Aunt Winnie, this tree's got its own love story. Two people were supposed to meet under it, but a snowstorm hit, and the guy had to be on the midnight train, and that was the end of that."

"Isn't that a song? Gladys Knight right? Figures you'd cite a love song for support." He made the woo-woo sound from the chorus of *Midnight Train to Georgia*.

"Well, you are no Pip." She folded her arms across her chest. "Have you always been this cynical?" No wonder he was still single.

"Hey, it was train-related. It was funny, not cynical."

"Says you." She couldn't believe he could be so blasé about the whole thing. "It's a lovely story."

He sighed. "Not with the romantic locket again."

Flummoxed, she let out a huff. "Don't judge. It could be something special."

"Or a dime store locket that someone threw away, or gave their granddaughter to wear, and she lost it on the playground."

"Go ahead. Make fun," she said. "I want to find the owner, or at least a family member."

He rolled his eyes. "How are you going to do that?"

"It's a small town. Someone would have to recognize these people," she said, realizing she was sounding a little defensive.

"Now, you're getting all googly-eyed over the whole idea of hunting them down?"

"Think what you want." She went back to decorating the surrounding bushes with ornaments, but she couldn't stop glancing toward the spot where she'd found the locket. Something about it tugged at her. The tree, the initials, the date. That piece of jewelry wasn't a cheap trinket either. It was a breadcrumb from a story waiting to be told.

When they finished decorating, dusk had draped South Hill in shades of rose and golden orange. The dogwood shimmered beneath a feathery light net of tiny white lights, every branch glittering as if it remembered being part of something important.

CHAPTER EIGHT

The next day, Nate pulled into the parking lot in front of Dogwood Hall after lunch, in response to Hannah Leigh's text that had read only: *Need a hand. Bring muscles and an open mind to the dogwood.*

He spotted her before the engine even cooled. She was standing near her SUV, sawhorses flanking a wide plank of painted wood that caught the winter light. Her hair lifted in the light breeze, and she had that determined set to her shoulders. The one that said she'd already made up her mind, and the rest of the world would have to catch up.

Smudges of green and ivory streaked her gloves, and a little crescent of paint marked her cheek like a badge of creativity. The scene looked more like a pop-up art fair than a parking lot. A thermos sat nearby, steam curling faintly from the lid, and the air carried the mingled scents of cedar, cold pavement, and fresh paint.

He climbed out, tucking his hands in his jacket pockets as he walked toward her. "Should I even ask?"

She glanced over her shoulder, eyes bright, the corner of her mouth lifting. "Just in time. What do you think?"

He came closer, the sign's bold white lettering taking shape:

Love Left Behind Board

Meet Me at the Dogwood — A New South Hill Tradition

He let out a low whistle. "Well, I'll give you this—you don't think small."

She grinned, clearly proud. "Told you I was serious about finding the owner of that locket. And this is how we're going to do it."

He folded his arms, trying not to smile. "Couldn't you post a flyer like a normal person?"

"Where's the fun in that?"

He chuckled under his breath. There it was again. That spark she carried, the one that made even the simplest idea feel like it might turn into something magical. He wasn't sure whether to be impressed or worried. Probably both.

She turned, one hand on her hip. "Besides, no one would even notice one of those. Have you seen the number of fluttering posters on the poles in this town?"

He shrugged. She had a valid point.

"I'm going to spread the word that people can post their love stories here. I've got a basket to hang on the side, and pushpins so people can tack them up if they want."

He could tell her mind was swirling with ideas.

"Maybe," she said, "we should write a couple of notes to get it started."

His brow shot up. "You mean make something up?"

"Of course not, but if you don't have one, you could write about someone else's story," she said. "Maybe one of them holds the key to who once wore this locket."

"What if it doesn't?"

"Well, *doubting Thomas*, once people get caught up in watching for new messages on the *Love Left Behind* board I can post the locket pictures here. With any luck, someone local will recognize those faces."

"I'm not doubting your plan, just asking questions." He could tell from her tone there'd be no talking her out of it. So instead, he picked up the sign. "I'm assuming this is what you wanted my muscles for. Where do you want this thing?"

"I've got the spot ready for you. Can you carry the sign by yourself?" she asked. "I can help."

"I've got it. Lead the way."

She started up the sidewalk, boots crunching over the frosted grass, a small cardboard box under her arm. The smell of paint and cold air mingled as they reached the edge of the lawn where the old dogwood stood, its branches bare but laced with twinkle lights that hadn't yet been plugged in.

"Right here," she said, pointing to a patch of softened earth.

He crouched to inspect the spot. She'd already prepped the holes, neat and even. "You dug these yourself?" he asked, half impressed, half amused.

"Of course. I can handle a screw gun and a pair of posthole diggers." She pointed to two 4x4s on the ground. "Mr. Graham donated the posts."

"Nice of him," he said, smiling as he as he anchored it to the posts and eased the display into position. He steadied the frame while she knelt beside him, packing the soil with her gloved hands. Their shoulders brushed once, then again, the contact light but enough to make him aware of how close they were.

"There," she said, brushing off her gloves. "That should do it."

He gave the board a light shake. "Solid." The lettering gleamed against the winter gray, bold and hopeful. "Looks good. People will notice this for sure."

She stepped back beside him, tilting her chin toward the sign. "That's the idea. A place for folks to leave messages, memories, maybe even confessions. If that locket belonged to someone in love, maybe their story will find its way back here."

Nate studied her for a moment, admiring the way her eyes caught the light. She had that same unshakable faith his grandmother used to talk about—hope stitched right into her bones.

"Well," he said finally, "if faith and hard work can bring a story home, I'd say you've already stacked the odds in your favor."

Her smile came slow, soft, and sure. "Guess we'll see."

They stood there a moment longer beneath the dogwood, the night still and winter air cool, the painted sign gleaming between them like a promise.

He gave the sign a testing shake. "Sturdy. Nice work."

"Thanks for the help," she said, her smile lingering a beat longer than necessary.

"You're welcome." Nate stepped beside her, close enough that their shoulders brushed as they looked over the scene. The quiet hum of Main Street came alive around the corner. In a while, all the lights here at *Dogwood Hall* would come on with the timer and illuminate this area and the new Lost Love Board.

Hannah Leigh For a moment, it seemed like they'd built something that mattered, even if it was just a sign and a dream. went digging through the box and hung a basket of notecards and ink pens on the side from a small hook already there. "There we go."

He read the words on the front of the basket.

"Happiness Zone." "Tell us your tale!" "Love letters welcome!" "No names. No problem."

"Not bad," he said, nudging her lightly. "You've thought this through." Still seemed unlikely to work, but he wasn't about to say that.

"Thanks," she said with a soft smile. "This tree's carried that locket for years, like it knew one day the story would need to be told again."

He looked at her instead of the sign, a grin tugging at his mouth. "Pretty sure this tree just found its headline," he said. "Unless the mayor shows up. My Uncle Clarence has opinions about everything from garland symmetry to bulb wattage. I'm guessing this didn't go through his approval committee?"

She shook her head, smiling. "I told you I came up with this idea last night."

He winced playfully. "Well, brace yourself. That's not gonna earn you any points."

"Oh, please." She tipped her chin toward him. "Let me guess. The mayor likes his trees like he likes his coffee. Bitter, plain, and best enjoyed alone."

"Ha. Good guess." Nate laughed, the sound echoing

down the sidewalk. "You're not wrong."

And right on cue, the man himself strolled up the sidewalk, hands clasped behind his back, scarf knotted tight as a necktie.

"Well, well," Mayor Collier said, eyeing the sign with angst. "Happiness zone? I see y'all have taken some creative liberties."

From where Nate stood, Hannah Leigh's smile was sunshine and mischief rolled into one. "Just making spirits bright," she said, and even Clarence's scowl seemed to lose some wattage.

The mayor gave a single "hmph," muttered something about city code, and kept walking.

As Uncle Clarence cleared the corner, Nate blew out a breath. "Honestly, that went better than I expected."

Hannah Leigh planted her hands on her hips. "A code violation? It's Christmas."

"That's my uncle. He's been allergic to joy since I was a kid."

"Well it's time someone reminded him what it feels like," she said, tapping her coat pocket where the locket rested. "Doubt he'd appreciate something as romantic as love letters or lost lockets."

"You think a locket's romantic?" Nate asked, teasing.

"You don't?"

"Me?" He kept his face as straight as he possible "I'd never argue with romance."

She gave him a look that said she wasn't buying it. "Sure you wouldn't."

"Okay, so kidding aside. How is this sign going to help

you find the owner of that locket?"

Hannah Leigh looked hesitant but then pulled a paper sign from the box she'd carried over. "This."

She pinned it at the top, smoothing it flat. "See. It says, '*Share your favorite hometown romance story, or a love you never got to say goodbye to.*'"

Not exactly subtle. "You think this will work?" He stepped back to take in the whole thing.

"I do," Hannah Leigh said. "People love to share stories. Especially when they think no one is listening. And if it doesn't work, I'll bake shortbread cookies shaped like hearts and sit here to lure folks in."

"Maybe that should be Plan A." Nate couldn't help teasing her. It was like sixth grade all over again. That odd sensation when you like someone, but don't know if they like you. "I actually think this is charming. We should spread the word down at the theater and at Bringleton's tomorrow."

"You'll help?"

"Wouldn't miss it," he said. "Let's pack up and get out of here." He couldn't help watching her.

She lingered by the sign, brushing her fingers across the bark of the dogwood like she was half-listening for its secrets.

He didn't know what story the locket carried, but the way she looked at it made him believe it mattered. He hadn't meant to hurt her feelings, but he could tell she was a little miffed. "You know, you have a point. The locket might be more than a coincidence." A soft breeze carried the smell of kettle corn and cinnamon, tugging her gaze toward the square.

"Thanks for saying that."

"Smell that? Best kettle corn around. Come on, my treat." Nate nodded toward the end of the block. "Looks like they're testing the sound system and lights down at the Colonial Theater."

Hannah Leigh smiled, falling into step beside him. "You mean South Hill's first miracle of the season?"

Nate arched a brow. "Funny, I thought the first one showed up wearing red boots with paint on her hands earlier today. Which would make the lights the runner-up."

Her laugh came without warning, light and genuine, the sound that made people turn and smile. He did too—because there was something about her that he couldn't look away from.

"You're impossible."

"Persistent," he said, grinning, eyes catching the light just right to make his teasing feel like a promise.

She shook her head, still smiling. "Let's stick to one miracle at a time. I'll take a rain check on the kettle corn. I'll catch up with you tomorrow."

CHAPTER NINE

The next day was the deadline for the vendor's festival paperwork. She went through each sheet and began assigning location spots to keep similar businesses separate and a good mix of crafts, food, and merch on every block.

Aunt Winnie stopped by her desk to check on things.

"I've only got a few forms with missing information, and it looks like we might be short a few junction boxes for all the ones requesting power." Hannah Leigh put all the problematic paperwork into a folder and handed it to her aunt for follow-up.

"You've been so helpful already," Aunt Winnie said. "I'm so glad you could come. I'd be running in circles without you. Tonight is the feature movie. You won't want to miss it. I've already left your ticket at the box office."

"You didn't have to do that. I could've bought a ticket."

"It's my pleasure. I have to give you some kind of bonus."

HOLIDAY CLASSIC MARATHON
FEATURING *CHRISTMAS JOY*
BASED ON THE NOVEL BY
LOCAL AUTHOR NANCY NAIGLE

The letters shouted the news in cheerful red and green,

framed by garland and silver bells that jingled in the breeze.

Hannah Leigh slowed as she got closer, her breath catching in a smile. As a teenager, she'd spent countless December nights in that theater dreaming big dreams under these very lights. The marquee made South Hill feel like Hollywood when she was a little girl.

She tugged her scarf tighter as she stepped up to the ticket booth. "I think there's a ticket here for me. I'm Hannah Leigh Parker."

The teenager straightened his Santa hat, taking the job as seriously as any big-league gig. His grin was wide, proud, and a little nervous in that first-day way. "Miss Winnie left your ticket." He practically glowed. "Enjoy the show."

Hannah Leigh couldn't help smiling. He had the same small-town pride she'd grown up on.

Inside, the lobby vibrated with Christmas cheer, every corner touched by sparkle and care. White ribbons trimmed in silver trailed down the grand staircase, magnolia leaf wreaths decked every door, and a velvet rope corralled a line of wide-eyed kids wearing faux reindeer ears and antlers waiting to take photos in front of a cardboard sleigh. The aroma of sweet and salty snacks wafted across the space.

Across the way at a folding table beside the concession stand, Hannah Leigh watched Birdie empty her entire purse across the table in a bit of a tizzy.

"I swear on my first husband's El Camino, it was here a minute ago!" She dug through a kaleidoscope of lipstick tubes, and at least three mini flashlights. "I had a bag of Pearl's Pralines."

"You sure you didn't eat them?" asked the teenage

concession girl. "They are hard to resist."

Birdie straightened, one hand on her hip and her Santa pin flashing. "Child, I don't eat pralines before a movie. It gums up my commentary. Besides, I planned to pass them out during the quiet part when the couple realizes they were in love all along."

Hannah Leigh couldn't stop herself. She crossed the room. "You mean the whole movie?"

Birdie whipped around and gasped as if she'd seen Elvis. "Well, well, if it isn't the prodigal Parker. I've been wondering, have you considered sticking around?"

"I'm just visiting," Hannah Leigh said with a smile, though Birdie's piercing stare made her feel like she'd just confessed to a federal crime.

Birdie hooked her arm through Hannah Leigh's. "Come sit by me. I have theories, and I need someone with sense to help me sort 'em out."

"Theories?"

"About something concerning our dogwood tree. It's famous, you know."

"I heard." Hannah Leigh blinked. "What about it?"

Birdie looked around, then leaned in like she was about to reveal something big. "Years ago, there was a story about a woman waiting for her true love under that tree." She straightened, lifting her chin the way she did when she was getting ready to get bossy. She folded her arms across her chest. "And now you're telling me you found an old locket buried underneath it? Coincidence? I don't think so."

"Actually...I didn't tell you that." Hannah Leigh held Birdie's stare. "Matter of fact, I haven't told anyone. How did you even know?"

Birdie stood there blinking with no response whatsoever. Finally, she winked. "I heard right, didn't I?"

Hannah Leigh hesitated to answer.

Birdie rolled her eyes. "Oh, honey, I hear things. It's not eavesdropping if the good Lord puts you in the right place at the right time and gives you sharp ears and a reason to use 'em, right?"

"I'm not so sure that's how it works." Hannah Leigh didn't agree, but the heat creeping up her neck gave her away. "It's probably nothing more than a trinket someone lost."

"Do you have it? I've got to see it." Birdie sniffed like a detective on a case. "It's never just a trinket in South Hill, especially not if it came from Harper's Jewelry."

"Oh, I guess it could've come from there," Hannah Leigh said. "I hadn't even thought about that. I should stop by there tomorrow."

"So, you *do* have the locket." A flicker of excitement danced in Birdie's eyes. "Everything means something here. Always has, always will. I believe the locket you found connects to that story from long ago.

Hannah Leigh hesitated, but despite her better judgment, she handed over the locket.

Birdie leaned in, curiosity glittering brighter than her rhinestone glasses. Suddenly, her mouth dropped open. "Well, I'll be. This is something." She slid her glasses down to the tip of her nose and squinted at the tiny photographs. "There's something familiar about these two…" Her expression pinched.

"There is?" Hannah Leigh's excitement was barely containable.

"Or maybe not," Birdie said, lowering her glasses with a *tsk*.

Her heart deflated like a balloon at a county fair that'd lost its helium halfway home. "So, you don't recognize them?"

"Nope," Birdie said brightly, already whipping out her phone. "But don't worry, Facebook will."

Before Hannah Leigh could stop her, Birdie was snapping photos like a woman on a mission.

"Whoa, Birdie! What are you doing?"

"Investigating," she said without a second glance. "This will be Exhibit A. I'm going to post the picture and spread the word."

"Don't you dare post that on the internet. Give me a chance to find her. This might be a very special treasure. The whole world doesn't need to be in on this."

"Don't worry, I'll only send it to my top-secret committee."

"You mean the gossip chain?" Hannah Leigh asked. "Please don't do that."

Birdie's lips pursed like she'd been told Santa was on strike. Then, simply turned and walked into the darkened theater.

Hannah Leigh stood there, surprised that Birdie didn't have to have the last word. Someone tapped Hannah Leigh's shoulder. She whipped around to see Aunt Winnie standing behind her.

"You scared me," Hannah Leigh said. "I didn't know you

were coming tonight."

"I'm not staying. Pressing Chamber matters require my attention, but I promised Birdie I'd tell you to sit with her. She's saving you a seat."

"Oh, I already talked to her. In fact, you just missed her."

"Doesn't matter. She'll have a fit if you don't sit with her, and blame me for it. Please do me a favor and sit with her. You won't even have to talk to her while the movie is playing. Even Birdie follows that rule."

With a resigned shrug, Hannah Leigh agreed.

Aunt Winnie said, "She always sits on the left, about six rows back from the screen. You'll see her."

"She was wearing antlers earlier with lights on them. Shouldn't be hard to spot her."

"Well, no one has ever accused Birdie of having good fashion sense. I've got to run, honey. Have fun." And with that, Aunt Winnie swept out of the building.

She made her way into the dimly lit theater.

In the middle of it all was Birdie, antlers flashing red and green atop her fiery curls, looking as proud as a Christmas parade float.

"Saved you a seat, sugarplum!" she called, patting the spot next to her like it owed her rent.

"You know you can't wear that flashing headband during the movie," Hannah Leigh said.

"I know. I wanted to be sure you could spot me." She removed the crazy headwear and shoved it into her tote bag, which now glowed on the floor like an alien.

Before the lights dimmed, Birdie leaned in. "Now, I don't mean to stir up mystery during a Christmas movie, but it's about the locket."

Hannah Leigh nodded cautiously.

"Well. I've been *thinking*." Birdie's whisper wasn't a whisper. It was a stage voice with the volume turned to 'nosey neighbor in a soap opera.'

"What if that locket belonged to someone the mayor was in love with before he married Elaine? Someone who is back in town now after all these years. What if," she lowered her voice dramatically, "he meant to propose to her at Christmas… but something stopped him. *And* then she left town, and he married Elaine. Like a rebound."

"Birdie," Hannah Leigh started, but Birdie was already rolling.

"No, no, listen to me. He's been grumpier than usual since you found that locket. And did you know he acts like he hates Christmas, but he sneaks into this movie every year, sits in the balcony, and pretends he's checking lightbulbs or something?"

"There's got to be a tender spot in him somewhere," Hannah Leigh offered. "Elaine died this time of year, didn't she?"

"Well, yes, but he is anything but nostalgic, and she died a long time ago. He's a grump. Honey, the man once canceled the Christmas parade because it interfered with deer hunting season. He is *not* sentimental. But guilt? *Regret?* Now *those* are powerful motivators." She tapped her temple with a candy cane stick. "Mark my words. That locket is a ghost from the mayor's past. And we're about to watch him unravel like a dollar store garland."

Hannah Leigh couldn't help glancing up at the balcony,

where a shadowy figure slipped into the back row and sat alone.

Was Birdie psychic, or just that good at solving mysteries?

The film started rolling, and the crowd from the lobby filled the theater.

Birdie leaned over once more and whispered, "Mark my words, sugar. That locket is the first thread in a whole quilt of secrets. A long-buried story. Mark my words." She rustled in her seat and leaned closer. "And you and that handsome carpenter are gonna be the ones to stitch it all back together. Well, with my help, of course."

Hannah Leigh bit back a smile. *Birdie and her prophecies.* She never met a whisper she couldn't turn into a headline. Still, something in the older woman's certainty tugged at her, a tiny spark she wasn't ready to name.

"Let's not start stitching just yet," she said lightly, hoping her grin sounded steadier than she felt. "But thank you for the vote of confidence."

Birdie winked. "Honey, it's not confidence. It's experience."

Hannah Leigh laughed under her breath, though her heart gave a small, traitorous flutter. Turning her gaze back to the flickering screen, she pretended to study the opening frames.

But Birdie's words lingered, settling somewhere between her ribs and reason. Maybe it was holiday magic, or maybe the woman's instincts weren't so far-fetched after all.

"A long-buried story," she murmured, more to herself than to Birdie. "You really think so? The two people pictured in that locket seem perfectly charming to me."

"You don't have my years of experience," Birdie said, straightening her shoulders. "You and Nate make quite the couple too, if you ask me. Now, shush. It's impolite to talk during a movie."

She didn't appreciate being scolded, since Birdie had been the one who started the conversation to begin with. That old woman was about as subtle as a firecracker in a quiet church, but she had excellent intuition.

The song 'Sleigh Bells' played as the opening credits of the movie rolled.

She'd just nestled down in her chair when someone walked down the center aisle carrying a box of popcorn and took a seat two rows up. She'd know the silhouette of that person anywhere. Nate. The carpenter, as Birdie put it.

And even all the Christmas cheer couldn't squash the niggling in Hannah Leigh's gut about what Birdie had said. Especially the part about her and the carpenter, because that was a little terrifying.

CHAPTER TEN

You were never too old to love movie night at the Colonial Theater. Hannah Leigh still adored the way sound filled every corner of the century-old theater and how no one minded a little whispered commentary. But tonight, even that warm hum of nostalgia couldn't quiet the restless beat in her chest.

When the final credits rolled, she lingered, not quite ready to face the man sitting a few rows ahead. Aunt Winnie had been right—Nate wasn't the same boy she'd known as a teenager—but that didn't mean she was ready to trust her heart again. Especially with Birdie's words still buzzing around in Hannah Leigh's head.

She slipped out a side door into the crisp night air. The cold met her like a sigh, quiet and steady. Flakes drifted beneath the lamplight, slow and silver, twirling on a soft winter breeze.

"The first snowfall of the year," she whispered, tilting her face toward the sky.

Downtown South Hill looked ready for a Christmas card photo. Even the police station was in on the fun, decked out with antlers on the patrol car mirrors and a red nose on the grill. A box marked *Operation Christmas Cheer: Evidence Drop* overflowed with toys and coats. Somewhere down the block, a speaker played "Silent Night," its melody threading through the stillness.

"Hey, are you okay?"

The voice startled her, but she recognized it instantly. Nate.

She turned, forcing a smile. "Hey. I'm great. Just appreciating the view."

Under the lamppost across from Harper's Jewelry, he looked every bit the hometown Christmas card come to life with that easy grin curving beneath a trace of scruff, flannel collar turned up, and snow dusting his dark hair and broad shoulders.

"You marched out of the theater like someone said *Die Hard* was the best Christmas movie," he teased.

"No one dared," she said. "But the praline-to-popcorn combo was my undoing."

"Then you need hot cocoa. The smallest size. Doctor's orders."

"You're a doctor now?"

"Only when the prescription's chocolate. And that I have two cups in hand already didn't hurt." He handed her one.

"Fair enough." She sat beside him on the frosty bench. From there, the LOVE sign rose in the distance by the railroad museum, the metal L still shaped from an old train crossing. "Were you waiting for me?"

"More like hoping to cross paths again." Nate looked away for a moment. "I've been thinking about the locket. Do you really think someone buried it there a long time ago?"

"Hard to say," she said. "Remember how rain used to wash down that hill? Mud could have hidden and uncovered it a dozen times over the decades."

"True."

"Birdie overheard us talking about it," she added with a grin. "She must've caught part of it while stringing garland by the front doors. Now she's made it her holiday mission to help solve the mystery."

He groaned. "She's got the best heart, and the worst boundaries."

"I think she means well."

"She *means headlines*."

"True." For a moment, the air between them warmed.

When she met his eyes, the notion she'd been chasing vanished clean out of her head. Heat climbed her neck before she pulled herself together. "Would you—uh—help me figure it out?"

"You mean, become your co-conspirator in Christmas sleuthing?" Nate teased.

"Exactly. Because if Birdie gets involved, this thing will be national news by Thursday."

Nate smiled, slow and sure. "I was hoping you'd ask."

That old flutter stirred in her chest again—light, stubborn, impossible to ignore. She blamed the cocoa. Definitely the cocoa.

"Where do we start?" he asked.

"I'll talk to Aunt Winnie," she said. "She might recognize the couple in the photos. They look old. Like *really* old."

"The photos could have faded over the years. Heat. Moisture. All that. Hard to say."

"Either way, I'd love to return it to the family. Especially at Christmas."

"I'm in," he said easily.

His agreeableness caught her off guard. "Tomorrow morning I've got to help at the Chamber with stuffing Santa's Secret Race gift bags."

"I've been dying to know what that is this year," he said. "Are you entering?"

"Not if I can help it."

"I always do," he said proudly. "Last year it was a cocoa chug with oven mitts. A fourteen-year-old beat me. Kid's a legend."

"What did he win?"

He gave her a mock look of offense. "Does it matter? An '*I Survived the Cocoa Chug*' shirt and a year's supply of marshmallows. Which just so happens is four jumbo bags."

"That'd last me a decade."

His laugh came low and easy. "I'll skip the race this year to help you with the gift bags, and afterward, coffee is on me. We'll figure out this mystery together."

That caught her by surprise.

He moved backward, hands in his pockets, smile lingering like an afterthought. "Glad you came home, Hannah Leigh." Then he turned and walked away.

By the time she found her voice to say *me too*, he was already gone.

It was late, and this trip had caught her off guard right and left. She'd worked so hard to avoid Nate after the movie only to have to face him out here in the dark alone. She might have been better off just letting things be amicable at the theater.

Doubting myself won't get me anywhere, and Nate doesn't deserve this much thought. He was a childhood crush. It's the past, and I'll be gone before I get to know the grown-up Nate anyway.

She made a dash for her truck, the heater groaning to life. Headlights tunneled through the night, the road unspooling before her like a dream she half-remembered. South Hill at its winter best—quiet, familiar, tender around the edges.

When she reached Aunt Winnie's, frost silvered every surface, making the holiday lights along the porch shimmer brighter. She'd always loved how her father used to drive them through town to admire the decorations. They'd been gone almost eight years now, and the ache never fully left. Especially not at Christmas.

On the porch steps, the air scented with wood smoke. Inside, the comforting aroma of Aunt Winnie's beef stew welcomed her home. A note on the kitchen counter read, *Help yourself, sweetheart.*

She served herself a bowl of it and sat at the kitchen table. Through the bay window, the tall pines stood like guardians, branches dusted in white. The sight tugged a smile from her.

She cradled the bowl in her hands, savoring the stew's warmth as her mind wandered back to the locket. She pictured it lying on the table—the way the faint light would catch on its worn edge, gold softened to bronze from years underground. In her mind, the clasp opened easily now, revealing two black-and-white portraits smiling out, faces preserved in miniature, waiting for someone to remember them.

Maybe the locket hadn't been a token of romance after all. Maybe it was a family's heirloom, a keepsake waiting for the right hands to hold it again.

She imagined her own grandparents' faces in its place and the ache of how much she'd give for even that small connection to her roots.

The locket didn't seem lost anymore, but patient, as if waiting for the right moment, and the right heart, to tell its story.

Discovering it at Christmastime seemed like more than chance. The past had found its listeners, and maybe, just maybe, so had they.

CHAPTER ELEVEN

The moment Nate stepped through the back door of the Chamber of Commerce, the smell of coffee and peanut butter cookies hit him square in the face. Not a bad way to start the day. Ever since Winnie had taken over as Executive Director, even these last-minute early morning meeting requests had perks.

She treated him like her resident handyman—part muscle, part moral support—and he didn't mind one bit. Winnie had a way of leaving her touch on everything from décor to morale. She'd even started casual Fridays, which still made his uncle mutter under his breath.

The office already hummed with activity despite the winter morning's hush outside. Because of the weather, schools and a few businesses delayed opening by two hours. Didn't bother him much. He kind of enjoyed being the guy who could still make it in, four-wheel drive and all.

"Morning," he said to Penny at the front desk. She'd worked beside Aunt Winnie for years, the quiet engine that kept the Chamber running. While others took credit for smooth events and tidy records, Penny was the one who made it all happen—efficient, unflappable, and armed with a color-coded planner that rivaled Santa's list. Behind her, the overnight snow clung to the windowpanes, frosting the view of South Hill in white.

At the heart of it all sat Winnie behind an oversized desk probably as old as she was. With a stack of flyers in one hand, and the phone under her chin, she juggled the tasks like a maestro, looking up long enough to flash Nate a bright smile that somehow said *good morning* and *don't track slush on my clean floor*.

He hopped back on the mat by the door, stomping the ice from his boots, and gave her a thumbs up, which granted him an approving nod. Before he said a word, Hannah Leigh stepped out from the side office, cheeks flushed from the cold and something more. In one hand she held the small velvet pouch he instantly recognized. She gave him that look, the one that said 'come on, back me up on this,' and he hustled over to her side and fell in step as she approached her aunt.

As soon as Winnie hung up the phone and took a breath, Hannah Leigh dove in.

"Aunt Winnie," she said quickly, "before Birdie tells half of South Hill, you need to hear this from me."

"Oh, dear." That brought Winnie to full attention. She turned her back on the phone and braced both hands on the desk. "Well, land sakes, child. That sounds serious."

"Well, it's not a bad thing. Not a problem with the festival or anything like that." Hannah Leigh drew a breath. "Yesterday, while Nate and I were decorating around the dogwood, I found something." She glanced over at Nate, and he gave her an encouraging nod.

"It rolled under my foot when I stepped in the dirt beneath the tree. It's an old gold locket with a man and woman's photograph inside. Nate was with me, but Birdie must've overheard us talking about it, because she asked me about it, and we hadn't told a soul."

Nate nodded to show his agreement with Hannah Leigh, but Winnie's brows shot straight up.

Winnie's tongue clucked. "Figures. That woman's got ears like a church bell. She can hear gossip hit the floor before it even leaves the preacher's lips."

Nate bit back a grin. She was right. If nosiness were an Olympic sport, Birdie Horn would have more gold than Michael Phelps.

And as if someone cued her to come on stage, the door banged open, and Birdie barreled into the office like a candy cane in a wind tunnel.

"You're not gonna believe what I heard over at The Doughnut Den!" she declared, eyes sparkling, and her cheeks as bright red as her hair.

Hannah Leigh and Nate exchanged a glance, half-amused, half-resigned.

"Good morning to you, too, Birdie," Hannah Leigh said.

"Morning," Nate echoed, leaning against the wall. "What's the headline? But first, why is your coat covered in…is that confectioner's sugar?"

"Oh, goodness." She swept at the mess, then stomped the ice off her bright pink and black boots and plopped into the nearest chair in the lobby with a dramatic sigh, as though she'd rehearsed this very moment. "Not my fault. The Doughnut Den has a new North Pole Puff, and I tried it. Actually, I tried three of them. My Lordy, light-as-air doughnuts dusted in powdered sugar and filled with whipped peppermint, and if St. Peter's handin' them out at the pearly gates, I'm ready to go now!"

Everyone laughed, and of course, that just egged old Birdie on, because if there was anything she loved more than doughnuts, it was being the center of attention. "Although that's not even the big news." She lowered her voice to a conspiratorial whisper. "Edna Sue swears she's seen that picture from the locket before. I showed her a photo on my phone, and Lord help us, she about slid right off her chair. Said she recognized that fancy collar from some newspaper clipping back in the sixties. She's been movin' all those dusty old microfiche files to digital, bless her heart, and now she's on a mission to help us figure out the mystery. Probably just wants some attention."

Aunt Winnie jumped in. "If that's not the kettle calling—" but someone interrupted her.

"Hey, I'm just being a good citizen, trying to help a neighbor," Birdie defended herself. "You know where the South Hill Historical Society is, Nate. Take Hannah Leigh over there quick before Edna Sue digs up half the archives on her own and calls Channel 7 about it."

"Sure," he said, happy to have an excuse to spend more time with her.

"You already showed the picture around?" Hannah Leigh's eyes darted to Nate, panic breaking through her calm.

He shrugged. Birdie was nothing if not bold.

Birdie's face went red. "Just trying to help."

"I didn't ask for your help," Hannah Leigh snapped, which struck Nate's funny bone. No one *ever* asked for Birdie's help. Never stopped her.

"Well, you would've. I don't mind. Look, a young couple vanished right before Christmas over sixty years ago. It had the whole town buzzing until the mayor at the time hushed it up."

Hannah Leigh's coffee cup stilled halfway to her lips. "Disappeared?"

Birdie nodded, her grin as wide as the Chesapeake. "Poof. Everyone assumed they'd eloped, but there was never a wedding, no postcards, no sightings. Just gone."

Nate caught the flicker of excitement in Hannah Leigh's eyes about where this was heading.

"Sounds like we need to make a trip over to the Historical Society," he said.

Birdie clapped her mittened hands in triumph. "Yes! You'd better. And when you find the scoop, remember who called it first. I expect front-page credit."

Winnie chuckled, shaking her head as she reached for her phone again. "Mercy, Birdie, if curiosity were cash, you'd own the whole county by now."

The office settled back into its steady buzz, but for Nate the morning had shifted. The locket, and the story sealed inside, wasn't only a mystery waiting to be solved. It was a reason to spend more time with Hannah Leigh, and that filled him with a hopeful, restless breath that seemed a lot like possibility.

"Ready to see what we can dig up?" he asked.

"Lead the way," Hannah Leigh said, her eyes bright.

He slipped his hand under her elbow, and together they ducked out the side door.

The narrow brick walkway led to the South Hill

Historical Society housed in the red brick building trimmed in creamy limestone, arched windows with carved keystones. The deep slate roof punctuated by an old copper finial still shone like a penny in the winter sun. Cast-iron lanterns flanked the heavy double doors, their frosted glass panes etched with delicate scrollwork. Above them, shiny gold leaf lettering spelled out *South Hill Historical Society* in elegant script.

"I never appreciated the beauty of the architecture of this building before." Hannah Leigh looked up, her eyes following the steep roofline.

The decorations on the building matched the era of the architecture. Garlands of dried oranges and fragrant cinnamon sticks twined along the wrought-iron railings. From the central arch, a wreath of antique sleigh bells tied with a strip of fancy velvet ribbon hung.

Nate held the brass handle for Hannah Leigh. "Welcome to the archives," he said with a grin.

CHAPTER TWELVE

The door of the South Hill Historical Society creaked open, releasing a breath of cedar-scented warmth. Inside, time seemed to roll back a century. This building was historic in itself.

Hannah Leigh sucked in an audible breath when they stepped inside. "I've always liked old pressed-tin ceilings. I love how they reflect the Christmas lights."

"Pretty, isn't it? I built that walnut display case over there." He didn't mean to brag, but it was one of the best pieces he'd ever crafted. It had taken months to complete. Now, the shelves held leather-bound ledgers that stood like sentinels guarding the town's architectural history.

"You did? Wow." She walked over, running her hand across the smooth surface. "I didn't know you made actual furniture. This is a big step from framing houses and putting up Christmas lights."

"You've been gone a long time."

"True," she said, tucking a strand of hair behind her ear and avoiding his gaze.

He watched her for a beat, a quiet smile tugging at his mouth. "Yeah," he breathed. "We've all learned a few things in fifteen years."

He enjoyed the way she absorbed the black-and-white photographs that wrapped the room in history. Steam engines puffing into the old station, Sunday parades down Main Street, and children waving from the schoolhouse steps. Each image, framed in dark wood, marched in perfect order along the walls like a silent gallery of South Hill's story.

He wasn't sure if it was his heartbeat or the old regulator clock ticking steadily on the mantel. More than once since Hannah Leigh had hit town, his heart had made itself known.

Near the front desk, a live Christmas tree stood like a tribute to Christmases past. Its short-needled boughs held tiny vintage train cars, silver sleigh bells, and sepia-toned photographs trimmed in gold cord. Cranberry-red velvet ribbons swept through the branches like soft trails of memory.

Hannah Leigh leaned closer, eyes tracing the photo of Main Street in the winter with the old theater marquee bright in the background. She wondered if Nate saw the similarities between that picture and last night.

"This place is incredible," she whispered, her voice instinctively soft in the reverent hush.

Nate smiled, watching wonder bloom in her eyes. "When I was a kid, my dad used to drag me here for paperwork, and I thought it was the most boring place in the world."

"Then you grew up," she teased. "Or, wait. Have you really?"

"Funny," he said, shaking his head. "I've been doing repairs here for a few years. Anytime I take on a historic renovation around town, I have to come here for sign-off. The blue-haired ladies who run this place? Don't let their age fool you. They're smart and tough as nails. They'll debate paint colors like they're guarding state secrets."

Hannah Leigh grinned. "Looks like they understand what they're protecting, by the looks of this place. This is beautiful."

He nodded, pride settling warm in his chest. "South Hill loves to remember where it came from." He glanced toward the archives room. "Maybe we'll find a clue about that locket. And if we don't..." He caught her gaze. "I can't think of better company for a wild goose chase."

Her breath hitched just slightly before she smiled. "Me too. I mean, it'd be nice to return this locket to the rightful owner."

The faint scent of lemon polish mingled with the age of the place.

Behind the counter, Nate spotted a familiar figure and lifted a hand. "Hi, Edna Sue. Have you met Winnie's niece?"

She stood. "Don't know that I have, but Birdie mentioned you two might be coming over."

"Hannah Leigh Parker, meet Edna Sue Tuggle," he said warmly. "Edna Sue runs this place like a first-edition librarian. Every record cataloged, every story right where it belongs."

"You'd better believe it." Edna Sue bustled over, her silver-blue hair perfectly coiffed and glasses perched halfway down her nose. "Good to see you, sugar. Nice to meet you, Hannah Leigh." She gave Nate a playful wink. "And this one here's my favorite contractor. Nobody else in this county knows how to coax an old building back to life the way he does. He treats history as if it's still living."

Heat crept up Nate's neck. "Just doing what I love."

Hannah Leigh smiled at their easy rapport, then drew a small velvet pouch from her pocket. "I'm sure Birdie's already spun this into a headline, but we're hoping you can help us figure this out. This locket might be connected to a love story that started under the dogwood, and we're trying to piece together what really happened.

"Oh, I know that story." Edna Sue's eyes brightened as Hannah Leigh withdrew the locket and handed it to her. "Isn't that lovely?" She glanced up from the locket. "I couldn't see too much from the pictures on Birdie's phone, plus everyone was all huddled around trying to get a peek."

"So much for Birdie not showing that picture around." Hannah Leigh shook her head.

Nate stepped closer to Hannah Leigh, a consoling pat on her shoulder. "No one can slow Birdie down. Don't take it personal."

"I've seen that picture before. I'm almost certain of it," Edna Sue looked determined. "I've been prepping our microfiche for digitizing. So, I've been looking at a lot of pictures. It's been hours of cleaning and labeling every piece before we ship it out."

Nate gave a low whistle. "That's not a job. That's an endurance event."

"I like to consider it job security." She placed her hand on the counter. "Although at my age, the task might outlive me."

Hannah Leigh opened her palm so the initials on the locket caught the light. "Can you point us to where we should start looking?"

Edna Sue leaned closer. "Well, now... the time frame of those pictures, based on hair and clothing style, would probably be in the sixties. But Birdie's right. This *is* a mystery." She tilted the locket toward the light, then raised her finger. "That woman looks familiar, though. Let me grab a box..."

After a thoughtful pause, she disappeared into the back room and returned with a carefully labeled box. "This batch should be from around the same time period. I wish I could narrow it down more for you."

"This is helpful. Thank you so much. We don't mind looking. We know you're busy." Nate carried the box to a long wooden table. He and Hannah Leigh sat shoulder-to-shoulder, flipping through brittle clippings and yellowed pages. Her brow furrowed as she read, lips parting softly when she found something interesting. He tried to stay focused on the records, but she made it hard.

A moment later, Hannah Leigh froze. "Nate?"

"What is it?" He leaned in.

The photo in her hand showed a couple mid-dance at a holiday party. The man wore a dark suit. She was wearing a plaid dress with a fancy color and a twinkling brooch. Beneath it, the caption read: Local sweethearts Henry Bell and Ruthie Danvers attend the Chamber Christmas Dance.

"That's them," Nate said, tracing the caption with his thumb. "Ruthie Danvers and Henry Bell. RD plus HB."

"The same initials as the locket," she whispered.

They both sat back, the discovery hanging between them like something sacred.

"South Hill never forgets a story," Hannah Leigh

whispered. "It just waits for the right people to finish telling it."

Nate raised his hand and slapped hers in a high-five as they celebrated. His mouth went dry. "You think that's us? The right people, I mean."

"Yes." Her eyes lifted, a soft smile curving her lips. "You're staring."

"Maybe." A spark of mischief crossed his face. "Or maybe I'm soaking in some of that Christmas magic everyone keeps talking about."

Her blush rose like a slow sunrise, but she didn't look away.

He leaned in just enough for their shoulders to touch. "Are you hungry?"

"Yeah."

"Good. Take a picture of that," he said, holding the photo steady.

She snapped it and called to Edna Sue. "We think we've found something. Can we leave this box here for a bit? We'll be back after lunch to double-check a few things."

Edna Sue answered quickly, "No one else scheduled a visit to the archives today."

"You're the best," Nate said.

She smirked. "Remember that next time you try to haggle with me over my restoration fees. History shouldn't have to bargain, sugar."

He tipped an imaginary hat. "Yes, ma'am."

They stepped out into the bright winter air, with old stories and possibilities following them out the door.

"This is a good lead," Hannah Leigh said, her breath

puffing white. "I'm so excited. Now, I'm dying for one of those North Pole Puffs Birdie was raving about."

Nate grinned, already imagining the sugary glazed doughnuts and her laughter mixing. But as they crossed the street, his thoughts drifted. Henry and Ruthie lingered like a melody that hadn't yet found its ending.

Maybe the locket wasn't the only story waiting to be finished. And the words just tumbled right out his mouth. "Do you think it's a coincidence we were the ones to find that locket?"

Her expression was hard to read. Couldn't take it back now though.

He looked over at the woman who'd been making him smile lately.

She didn't answer right away. She stepped gingerly, her arms slightly out as if to keep from slipping. Either she hadn't heard him, was unwilling or too afraid to give it a moment of consideration.

He wanted to say it out loud, but the words never left his mouth. *Maybe we have a story to finish, too.*

CHAPTER THIRTEEN

Hannah Leigh sat across from Nate at the Doughnut Den surrounded by so much sweetness her teeth ached. No, she didn't believe in coincidences at Christmastime. Not in South Hill, where memories lingered and its small-town stories always eventually got told. She didn't think that locket was a coincidence, and neither was running into Nate.

With my luck, it was more like the devil tempting me into another relationship that'll end horribly.

And so she tried to pretend she hadn't heard him. So far, he seemed to be buying the act.

They had barely finished their doughnuts before she pulled out her notebook and started scribbling. Names. Places. Questions. The kind that didn't let go until you followed them to the end.

Her phone buzzed. "It's Birdie." She read the text to him.

BIRDIE: 411 on locket mystery that'll bake your biscuits.

"That's colorful." Nate shook his head. "She ought to trademark half the things she says."

"Oh, there's more coming." She waited patiently as the dot-dot-dots pulsed. "Here we go."

BIRDIE: Old post office has boxes of undelivered mail.

Nate leaned over her shoulder. "Do we even want to know what that means?"

"Probably not," Hannah Leigh said, grinning. "We aren't even finished running down her first lead."

"I got this." He lifted his phone out and dialed Birdie. "What is this text you sent to Hannah Leigh about undelivered mail?" He nodded, followed by a series of mm hmmm's and an eye roll. "Thanks. Okay, bye."

"What?" Hannah Leigh said before he even lowered the phone. "What did she say?"

"According to Birdie's cousin's neighbor's uncle—"

"Oh Lordy."

"Right? Yeah, well he was a mail carrier in the sixties, and he told her there are boxes of undeliverable mail from that time still stored at the old post office site," Nate said, half-grinning. "We can get the key from the realtor."

Hannah Leigh blinked, trying to process it. "Undeliverable mail? What are we looking for?"

"Well, Edna Sue told Birdie we might have a name for the woman in the locket. So, Birdie thinks we might find a piece of mail that never got delivered to Ruthie." Nate tilted his head, amused. "I agree. It's a stretch." He shrugged.

"I tell you what. People in this town spread gossip faster than I can live it. We just found that name." She glanced around the Doughnut Den, hoping no one was overhearing their conversation.

"I know. Birdie is something, and the mail thing feels like a long shot, even for Birdie, but what if…"

"It definitely has me curious," she admitted. "What are

you thinking?"

Nate angled closer, his eyes catching hers with a spark of mischief. "Looks to me like we're going to search through boxes of undelivered mail."

"And maybe find something from or to Ruthie or Henry," she said, though doubt colored her voice. She took another bite of her doughnut.

He snickered under his breath. "Not the proverbial needle in a haystack exactly, but pretty darn close. I'll check in with the guy who has the listing at the post office and see when we can get the key."

"I'll do some online searches and see what I can dig up," she said. "Speaking of Birdie and her hunches, she said something about your uncle being in love with Margaret Jane before he married Elaine. Do you know anything about that?"

"No, but he and Aunt Elaine were barely out of school when they married. I figured whatever came before was just young love—the kind that usually burns out fast."

She caught herself wondering if the pull between them was real—a spark that had never quite gone out—or the echo of what she'd been missing since Evan. The thought made her heart flutter, warmth and uncertainty tangling until she forced herself to breathe and look away.

"Birdie thinks the mayor's been acting off ever since we found the locket," Hannah Leigh said, her voice a touch steadier than she felt. "She's convinced he has some connection to it—maybe even through Margaret Jane, now that she's back in town." Hannah Leigh met Nate's eyes again. "What if Birdie's right?"

"She's right more than I'd like to admit, but I don't know—"

"About the locket," she clarified. "And the letters. Or the mayor? He *has* been cranky. Have you seen a difference in him since we found the locket?"

"He's always been a curmudgeon if you ask me. But if he knows about the locket, it's because Birdie told him. But the locket's timing doesn't fit. I doubt he'd have been buying gold lockets as a teenager."

"Right. 1964 is on the locket, plus the initials don't match. Could he have gotten it from a pawn shop?"

"Possible, but I don't know about this one." Nate exhaled through his nose, then muttered, "You know Birdie also thinks her cat communicates with ghosts."

"I hate to admit that doesn't surprise me." She couldn't help but smile. "I don't even know what to say about that but have to admit the mayor's been acting strange."

Nate said. "It's practically his brand."

"Does that run in your family?" Hannah Leigh tried not to smile, but the expression on his face tickled her. She hoped the comment about his uncle did not offend him. "I'm kidding. I couldn't resist, but seriously, she said something that stuck with me. She said guilt and regret were powerful motivators. And honestly? He's been a little weird with me. He barely looked at me at the Chamber meeting. Didn't even complain about the cocoa prices."

Nate froze. "Wait. He *didn't* complain about the price of the cocoa?"

"Not a whimper."

He paused, holding her gaze. "Okay, say Birdie's holiday

soap opera theory isn't completely off the rails. Then what?"

Hannah Leigh sighed and glanced away. "I wish I knew. She's spun so many wild ideas that I caught myself thinking it might be her locket and she's just reeling us in for entertainment."

"Now that would be something." Nate shook his head. "Birdie's highly intuitive, but I've never known Birdie to be tricky. It would be an unexpected twist."

Hannah Leigh shrugged. "Even if there's no big story, getting the locket back to a relative matters most. We're close now that we have those names. This could be a special Christmas keepsake to someone."

"I agree. And we have our RD and HB match." Nate's brow furrowed. "Maybe we start a list of other possibilities."

She grinned. "Should we skip the post office altogether?"

"I'm not saying I *believe* Birdie Horn," he replied, tugging his coat against the cool night air, "but I've learned to stop betting against her. I say we give it a one-hour glance. If we don't come up with anything, we shelve it. Deal?"

He stretched his hand to hers, she grabbed his, and they shook on the plan. "I'll text as soon as I get the key."

A flicker of something unexpected filled Hannah Leigh. This small-town mystery had cracked something open. Curiosity. Connection. Maybe even…chemistry.

CHAPTER FOURTEEN

The next afternoon, they stood in front of the old post office that had been shuttered for over twenty years. The wind whipped Hannah Leigh's hair across her face, and she hugged her coat tighter. "It's a little spooky, isn't it?" She had the heebie-jeebies already, and they weren't even inside.

"Afraid of ghosts?" Nate asked, deepening his voice and doing his best spooky impression.

Hannah Leigh crossed her arms, trying not to smile. "If that's your haunting voice, you'd never make it past orientation. You're a terrible Ghost of Christmas Present."

"Guess I'll stick to carpentry," he said.

"Good plan. Now, spiders and mice? That's another story."

"I can handle the critters," he said, grinning as he lifted a tarnished brass key. "Come on. It's just an old building full of forgotten moments."

The heavy door groaned open, echoing through the empty lobby. Inside, the air was cold and stale, thick with the smell of dust, wood oil, and old paper.

"Smells like something died in here," she muttered.

"Adds to the charm," Nate said, moving toward a stack of postal crates. "Old Mr. Dillard was the postmaster back when this place closed. The realtor said he was a real quirky guy. A hoarder who couldn't stand the idea of tossing anything, even federally regulated mail. So he boxed up all the undeliverables, and stuck them in the storage shed out back. They forced him to retire when they moved to the new building, and he died a month later. No one has ever bothered to go in and do anything with any of that stuff."

Hannah Leigh swept her phone flashlight across the dusty counters and rows of brass-front mailboxes with twisty combination knobs that no one ever seemed to master. "So, what? They moved what was important and left everything else behind."

"Yep. Out of sight, out of mind. Folks figured he'd handled it." Nate shrugged. "I'm pretty sure it wasn't common knowledge."

"Birdie found out."

"Well, she's more capable than the CIA." He walked through the space. "I would love to buy this place and turn it into something cool."

"Maybe one day you'll get your chance." Hannah Leigh shook her head, amused.

"Not likely," he said. "It's way overpriced."

"If South Hill is sentimental enough to give old mail a free twenty-year lease, I think there may be a chance they will eventually decide that building will be better off renovated than crumbling."

They rummaged through drawers of yellowed paperwork and brittle envelopes until she lifted a green envelope from the pile.

"Look. This letter's addressed to Santa Claus, South Pole. 'Forward to North Pole if Found' written on it."

Nate grinned. "On this hunt, I half expect it'll lead us there. Come on. There's not much left in here. The boxes are supposed to be in the storage shed out back."

She tucked the card in her pocket and followed Nate outside and down the cracked sidewalk.

He worked the key, and after only a brief protest, the shed door swung open. A string of jingle bells clanged wildly against it.

"Well, that's not creepy at all," she said. "Very festive for a ghost encounter."

A bird burst from the rafters, scattering dust. Hannah Leigh yelped, then gathered her wits. "Where did that come from?" she said, catching her breath.

"Don't panic. It's just a pigeon," Nate replied, scanning the rafters. "Or a bat in a holiday disguise."

"That thing was the size of a flying chihuahua wearing a feather boa," she insisted. "That was no bat."

Their voices bounced off the metal walls. The bird settled high on a beam, glaring down like a cranky landlord.

"Let's find the box before Big Bird decides we're lunch," Nate said.

Hannah Leigh was just thankful it wasn't a bat. Rabies would not be a fun way to spend the holidays. There were boxes stacked on floor-to-ceiling racks down each side and a row in the middle. She started reading the labels on the boxes, careful not to disturb any other tenants of the shed.

"Looks like they're organized by date," she said, brushing dust from the nearest stack. "Oldest on that side."

They split up, working quickly. Then Hannah Leigh found what they'd been hoping for half-buried beneath cobwebs. *Undeliverable Mail ~ 1964, South Hill 23970.*

Her breath caught. "Nate. Here! I found boxes with the same year as the picture of Ruthie and Henry Bell."

He hurried over and pulled them down. "Two of them. Let's take these inside and get them under some light."

"There's no power here."

"Oh, right?" Nate rubbed the back of his neck, a sheepish smile tugging at his lips. "My place is just up the block. We can go there."

Her pulse gave a little skip. *His place?* Her nod came quick to keep from changing her mind. "Sure. Yeah. Cool." She picked up a box, leaving the other for him to carry. "Following you."

Nate put the boxes in the truck and then gave Hannah Leigh a boost into the passenger seat. When he started the truck, he said, "I was just thinking about how old Ruthie had to have been. If she was say early twenties in 1964, then she'd be in her early eighties now."

"I hope she's in good health. She might not even remember if that locket ever belonged to her."

"Somehow, I don't think anyone ever forgets that kind of detail." Nate's pickup truck rumbled down Main Street, then turned the corner near Harper's Jewelry. After two more quick turns, Hannah Leigh knew precisely where he was going.

He slowed in front of the red-brick building with arched windows and worn painted lettering that read *South Hill Mercantile.* A wreath on the main entry and candles in every window, just like the old days.

"You live here?" she asked as they climbed out.

"Sure do."

"But it's huge."

"I live on the top floor," Nate said, hefting both boxes with ease.

"I can take one."

"Let me get this." He pushed the door closed. "Follow me," he said. "This building used to be the newspaper office a hundred years ago, before it was the mercantile. I restored it, refinished the floors, and added new windows. Tried to keep the history but make it modern enough to be livable. There was a lot of cool stuff in the attic still."

Inside, the stairwell creaked beneath their steps, the air carrying the faint scent of cedar and sawdust. Nate flipped the old iron latch and pushed open the door to his apartment, revealing a space that stopped Hannah Leigh in her tracks.

It stretched the entire second floor—wide-plank floors that gleamed under soft light, tall windows straight ahead spilling late-afternoon sun across an open-concept living space. Exposed brick lined one wall, and opposite it, a riverstone fireplace anchored the room, its walnut mantel rough-hewn and solid.

Built-in shelves framed the hearth, filled with framed photos, a few old woodworking tools polished to a satin glow, and a scattering of handmade Christmas ornaments arranged just so.

To the right, a large farmhouse table sat near the bank of windows, its surface dotted with blueprints and a half-finished mug of coffee.

Beyond that, the kitchen stretched along the far wall with gleaming white cabinets, open shelving with neatly stacked dishes, and a big copper sink that looked straight out of a home design magazine. A sliding barn door stood slightly ajar near the back, hinting at a bedroom or workshop beyond.

"I'm working on lease options for the ground floor," Nate said, balancing the boxes on his hip as he reached for the switch. Edison bulbs glowed to life, warming the space even more. "Trying to let the building pay its own way."

"Great idea," she whispered, still turning in place to take it all in.

He set the boxes on the table, glancing her way. "It's a lot for one person, but…" His tone softened, a quiet honesty threading through. "Maybe not forever."

She didn't trust her voice enough to answer. Instead, she ran a finger along the edge of the table. "You've got good taste," she said, hoping her voice didn't give her away.

He smiled at that, the kind that made her pulse skip. "Let's see what that crazy old postmaster Mr. Dillard left behind."

"That's a D initial. Did his first name start with an R? What if he's the RD on the locket?"

"That would be funny, but I don't think so. Hope not, anyway. We don't need another lead that might take us off this one." They pulled things out of the first box. Hannah Leigh untied the twine around a bundle of letters. The paper was thin, soft, and yellowed with age. "Look at these postmarks," she said. "1963… 1964… right around the holidays."

Nate whistled. "Old Dillard kept everything. Sadly, he was even worse at home. A hoarder, although back then I don't think anyone knew that was a thing. The realtor said, rumor had it when Dillard died, the EMTs couldn't even get into the house with the stretcher there were so many things piled up."

"Different times back then." She flipped through envelopes, then paused on one with smeared ink making it almost unreadable. She blinked, hoping she wasn't imagining it. It just seemed too easy. "This letter addresses Miss Ruthie Danvers," she said, squinting at the faded script. "We have her address. Is there a chance she still lives there?"

"That's unlikely, but it gives us a starting point. See what the letter says first."

"No return address, but the postmark is local." She tugged at the flap, but the paper resisted.

Nate flicked open a pocketknife and slid it beneath the seal. "There you go."

Hannah Leigh unfolded the paper. Her voice trembled just a little as she read aloud:

My darling, Ruthie,

Thank you for agreeing to wait for me beneath the dogwood the evening before Christmas Eve. You are too special to leave behind.

Don't tell a soul. We can't risk anyone trying to keep us apart. I must leave on the midnight train that night. Please come with me.

My job promises us a life of excitement that I can't imagine sharing with anyone else. I promise to always take care of you. Meeting you changed me. I can't be without you.

If you meet me, we will begin our life together. If you are not at the tree, then I'll know you changed your mind, and I promise to respect that.

Forever my love, Henry

Their eyes met, just for a second, but it was enough. Her breath caught. A chill came over her that had nothing to do with the draft whispering under the window.

She swallowed hard, then dug through the rest of the box with haste.

"Wait," she said. "This one's addressed to Henry Bell at the La Crosse Hotel. The postmark is the day after Christmas."

Nate leaned closer, brow furrowing. "La Crosse is only about four miles from here. The main train station was there back then. That must've been where he was staying for the newspaper story."

"Maybe it took her a few days to get out of the house," Hannah Leigh said, thinking aloud. "She's asking why he didn't show up in this letter." She turned the letter over gently. "We've got to find Ruthie."

"Winnie and Birdie didn't recognize the name," Nate said. "You'd think they'd know everyone within a hundred miles."

"She could've changed her name, or left for a while."

They sat in quiet awe for a moment, surrounded by the whispers of history. Then Nate exhaled, the corner of his mouth lifting. "Guess we just uncovered South Hill's greatest love story."

"Or its saddest," she mumbled. She took pictures of what they'd found and put the mail back in the box.

"Maybe both." He pressed his hands together. "Did you get pictures of everything?"

"Yes. We'll put all of this back right where we found it, so we don't end up in federal prison. That would be an even sadder story."

"You got that right. I don't think they serve Bringleton's cocoa or pralines in jail."

They repacked the boxes and carried them outside to Nate's truck and drove in silence to the post office to return the boxes where they had found them. As Nate stepped out of the shed next to Hannah Leigh, a gust of wind barreled down the alley and slammed the door with a bang.

Hannah Leigh jumped. "Okay, that felt personal."

Nate grinned. "You're wound as tight as a box of new Christmas lights." He locked the door.

She laughed a little too quickly. "Let's hope we don't short out." Truth was, she could feel the tension buzzing under her skin. The kind that came from too much thinking and not enough breathing.

Then fate, or maybe it was karma that rolled in, quite literally.

A blow-up snowman broke free from a yard display and came barreling across the sidewalk like a jolly tumbleweed. Nate lunged, missed by an inch, and Hannah Leigh caught the full brunt of its inflatable cheer.

She yelped as the snowman's puffy arms wrapped around her, sending her backward onto the damp ground with a soft thud. For a second, she sat there, tangled in white nylon and blinking up at the swirling flakes.

Nate raced over to help her up. "Are you okay?"

She brushed snow from her sleeve, half laughing herself. "Sure. Wrestling snowmen beside the maybe-haunted post office. Just another Tuesday in South Hill."

"Wednesday," he said, grinning.

Her eyes widened. "Then I've officially lost a day. That was one serious snowman roll."

Amusement flickered in his brown eyes. When he offered his hand, she took it—and felt her pulse skip.

For a heartbeat, the rest of the world fell away as if the snow, the street, even the ridiculous snowman deflating behind them. He looked at her like he saw *her*, not the version she tried to hold together for everyone else. And in that quiet, unexpected way, she felt seen.

"What's that look mean?" he asked, grinning.

"Nothing," she blurted. "Like you just rescued me from a runaway snowman."

"Yeah," he said with a teasing tilt of his head. "That's me. Your knight in Christmas flannel."

"Maybe something doesn't want us unraveling this mystery," she said, smiling despite herself. His grin sent her insides tumbling again.

"Just one more reason not to give up," he said.

As they stepped into the chill night, snow whispering underfoot, the air felt thick with untold stories. Ruthie's, maybe the mayor's, and perhaps her own. Each waiting for its turn to find a happy ending.

He drove her back to her car, and there wasn't a word

between them. "Here you go."

She climbed out then leaned in, her elbows on the seat. "I enjoyed getting to know you, I mean who you are now, and seeing where and how you live. It was a really good day."

"I'm looking forward to another one just like it tomorrow. Well, without the ghosts or runaway snowman."

"Deal." She watched him drive off, then tried to pull herself together to go back inside the Chamber of Commerce office to help Aunt Winnie with the challenge of the day. Turned out, she'd missed the tinsel garland getting sucked into the copy machine *and* Aunt Winnie catching Birdie trying to fix the shorted snowflake-shaped lights with a butter knife. Typical South Hill chaos. But somehow, they'd smoothed it all out and still made it home in time for a decent dinner before bedtime.

That night, long after she'd washed the dust from her hands and crawled into bed, Hannah Leigh couldn't stop thinking about those letters, or about Nate.

The way he'd handled each fragile envelope with such care, like every word mattered. The way his laughter had filled that drafty old post office until it didn't feel spooky anymore.

She told herself she'd come home to South Hill for a reset, not a rerun of her heart. But as she stared up at the ceiling, she couldn't shake the feeling that maybe the past wasn't the only thing waiting to be found here.

CHAPTER FIFTEEN

When Hannah Leigh stepped outside, it was like walking into a Christmas postcard. Flurries danced around them, dusting the nativity display in front of the bank and catching on her eyelashes with a tickle. The lamppost outside Harper's Jewelry wore a hand-knitted scarf and a big silver bow, and someone had tucked tiny stockings along the base, each with a handwritten name.

In the jewelry store window, warm white lights framed a single velvet box holding an antique ring that looked like it carried a century's worth of love stories. Hannah Leigh's heart pulsed with that hopeful, irritating ache that always snuck up on her this time of year.

Of course, that was when Aunt Winnie pulled up in her bright red convertible, top down, tartan cape trailing behind her like a Christmas banner.

"There she is!" Winnie hollered, climbing out with flair.

Hannah Leigh gaped. "What on earth are you doing driving that thing in this weather? You know Uncle Skip would be in a tizzy! He's got to be rolling over in his grave."

"Well, he's not here to do any fussing. God bless his heart. I miss him, but I make the rules nowadays." Winnie grinned and tugged her cape into place. "Besides, I kind of like driving this car with the top down in the cold."

Hannah Leigh's heart softened. Her aunt had taken a long

time to find joy again after losing Uncle Skip. Maybe a little convertible joyride in December was the type of crazy she'd earned.

"But why the top down?"

"Had to give a giant nutcracker a ride from the arena where they used it last night back to the square so he can guard the Christmas tree. Couldn't find a man with a truck, and I was in a hurry, so I had to improvise."

"Well, I guess in some odd way your gumption impresses me." *Am I doomed to be crazy? It's in Winnie's DNA. Same DNA as Mom's was.* A quote from an old sitcom came to mind.

This is the South. And we're proud of our crazy people.
We don't hide them up in the attic.
We bring 'em right down to the living room and show 'em off.

And wasn't Aunt Winnie proof of that right now?

"Carry on," Hannah Leigh teased.

Winnie slid her sunglasses down, eyes sparkling. "The mayor's got a sudden obsession with that *Love Left Behind* board. Tried to have it taken down, you know. Said it was inciting unrest."

"Unrest?" Hannah Leigh couldn't believe it. "It's a memory board, not a mutiny."

"Mmm-hmm. And yet, he's jumpier than a cricket on a griddle. You know what that means."

"That it's Christmastime and everyone's sleep-deprived?"

Her aunt arched a perfectly drawn brow. "That there's

something worth digging into. Which I intend to do, right between my cider tastings and wreath-judging duties."

Before Hannah Leigh could respond, her phone buzzed.

NATE: Meet me at the Love Left Behind Board. Top of hour?

She smiled despite herself, typing back a thumbs up and a clock.

As she slipped her phone away, her gaze lifted again to Harper's Jewelry's display window. Maybe it was time to follow up on that mystery, and on the pull in her chest that had nothing to do with Christmas nostalgia.

She pushed through the door, the little bell above it jingling like the start of a new chapter.

The bell's chime faded into the soft tick of the old grandfather clock in the corner. Harper's Jewelry looked almost exactly as she remembered, glass display cases lined with velvet trays, brass sconces casting a golden glow, and the faint scent of metal polish and cedar cleaner.

"Well, if it isn't Hannah Leigh," Sandra Kinker called from behind the counter, her silver hair swept into a perfect twist. "Wondered when you'd make time for me. You here for your aunt's bracelet repair or just to make a little trouble?"

"A little of both," Hannah Leigh said with a grin. "Actually, I was hoping you could help me with something."

Sandra peered over her glasses. "What've you got there?"

Hannah Leigh placed the locket on a square of black velvet. The gold oval looked even more delicate under the light.

"Well, I'll be," Sandra murmured. "That's *the* locket, isn't it?"

"*The* locket?"

"Honey, this looks an awful lot like the one that folks around here have told stories about for years. The dogwood tree story." Sandra then dropped the act of pretending she'd recognized it, and said, "Plus, Birdie already dropped some hints you'd be coming."

"Of course, she did."

"Gotta love her." Sandra motioned toward the workbench. "Victoria, come look at this."

Victoria hurried over, dark curls bouncing as she tugged on a jeweler's loupe. She leaned in, studying the hinge and edges with care. "There's a stamp on the clasp," she said after a moment. "That's Grandpa's mark. He used it on all his custom engravings beginning in the fifties."

"So it's from here," Hannah Leigh whispered.

Sandra nodded, nostalgia flickering in her eyes. "Definitely. I can go through the old ledgers to see if we can find who ordered it, but honestly that was a long time ago. Might take a bit. We've got eighty years of history in those books."

"If you find anything, would you let me know?"

"Of course, sweetheart," Sandra said, patting her hand. "If that locket has a story, it's about time we heard the ending."

Victoria snapped a quick photo for their records. "We'll keep you posted. If it turns out this locket is part of that dogwood legend, imagine what a story that would be. Great for the shop, and the town. We might actually get the

Hallmark movie made here. Your aunt has been writing letters for years trying to get them to bite. No luck yet."

As Hannah Leigh stepped back into the cold, the bell jingled behind her. The idea of holding the very locket from a decades-old love story was so romantic, like she was carrying a heartbeat that didn't belong to her.

Well, she'd confirmed the locket's roots in South Hill, but there wasn't much else to trace Ruthie Danvers and Henry Bell. She walked over to Dogwood Hall to meet up with Nate, and to see if maybe something new that could help was on the *Love Left Behind* board.

The venue was buzzing when she arrived, and the number of cards and notes on the *Love Left Behind* board had doubled overnight. She began reading them. Most were just silly things by people who just wanted to be a part of something, which was fine. It made her happy that it was an inviting thing to do. Some notes were heartbreaking, others funny, a few written in the shaky penmanship of second chances.

"You're late, Parker."

She turned to find Nate at her side, arms crossed, that familiar grin tugging at the corner of his mouth.

"Had to make a stop." She lifted her tote. "Harper's Jewelry. Turns out the locket came from there. Sandra recognized her grandfather's engraving stamp."

Nate gave a low whistle. "So the story's real?"

"Looks that way."

He leaned in, scanning the board. "Small towns and secrets. They are always more connected than they look."

They stood shoulder to shoulder, reading one note after

another, until one caught her eye. Plain white paper, printed in block letters:

A man beneath the dogwood.
A broken heart.
A promise gone unkept.

Hannah Leigh swallowed. "You think this is the same story? About Ruthie and Henry."

"Could be," Nate spoke with easy warmth. "Or maybe this tree's seen more heartbreak than we realized."

When she looked up, he was watching her. The quiet between them stretched, charged and uncertain, full of something she wasn't ready to name.

"You've got glitter on your cheek," he said, reaching to brush it away. His fingers grazed her skin, light as breath.

Her pulse jumped. "Hazard of the job."

His gaze went up and then dipped toward her lips. "Occupational perk for me."

The mistletoe hanging over the entryway caught her eye, and she took a step back. "Seriously?"

"Hey, I didn't put it there." He leaned a fraction closer, his breath warm against the cool air between them.

Her heart raced, and his breath warmed her cheek.

"Hey, Coach!" a voice hollered.

They broke apart like guilty teenagers. A kid in a football jacket jogged up, grinning. "Mom says to remind you I'm going to be late to practice tomorrow."

Nate exhaled through a laugh. "Yeah. Got it. No problem"

When the boy ran off, Hannah Leigh met his gaze again, trying not to smile too wide. "Timing's everything, huh?"

"Apparently, mine isn't as good as I thought." His eyes lingered on her for a beat longer than necessary. "We'll finish that conversation later."

CHAPTER SIXTEEN

Nate's parents taught him to trust his gut feelings. And right now, Nate's gut said this Ruthie Danvers woman held the missing piece to a love story that deserved better than rumors and half-truths.

By the next morning, he'd tracked down an address through one of his old coaching contacts whose aunt worked at the county assessor's office. A few phone calls later, he and Hannah Leigh headed toward Laurel Creek, the next town over, where Ruthie now lived at a place called The Camellia Residences.

It wasn't what he expected. The senior community looked more like a bed-and-breakfast than a care home. Brick buildings framed by porches and rocking chairs, with wreaths hung on every door and a camellia bush blooming pink against the frost.

Inside, the front desk nurse looked up over her glasses as they approached. Her name tag read *Gloria*.

"Morning," Nate said with that movie-star grin. "We were hoping to visit one of your residents. Miss Ruthie Danvers."

Gloria's eyes narrowed in that way that warned off both salesmen and snoops. "Are you family?"

"Not exactly," Hannah Leigh said. "We're helping with a town heritage project. There's an old story we're trying to confirm, and Miss Ruthie's name came up. We were hoping to ask her a few questions."

The nurse folded her arms. "Miss Ruthie doesn't get many visitors. She's sharp as a tack, but I don't want anyone upsetting her."

"Promise we'll be respectful," Nate said, sincerity steady in his voice. "If she's not up for it, we'll head right out."

Gloria hesitated, then sighed. "All right. Wait here."

A few minutes later, she reappeared, holding open a hallway door. "She'll see you. Follow me."

As they walked, Nate took in the space. It was bright, warm, and filled with little touches that made it feel like home. Handmade quilts hung in the hallways. Someone had placed poinsettias in every window.

"Pretty place," he whispered.

"Sure is," Gloria replied. "We like to keep things cheerful. Miss Ruthie's apartment even has a garden patio. She's our resident plant whisperer."

They stopped at a door near the end of the hall. Through the window, Nate glimpsed a tidy sitting area. The edge of Ruthie's patio held about every color of pansy he'd ever seen.

Gloria knocked, cracked the door. "Miss Ruthie? You have guests here."

"I do?" A moment later, a small woman appeared, her white hair swept back, her sweater a soft shade of rose. She studied them with bright, curious eyes. "Well, don't just stand there in the hallway," she said to them. "Come on in before you let the cold follow you."

The warmth hit him first, the kind that wrapped around a

person and made the air feel safe, but he was already getting too warm. Crocheted blankets hung folded across the back of the sofa.

"Ms. Danvers, ma'am," Nate said, holding out a hand. "My name's Nate Collier, and this is Hannah Leigh Parker. We're from South Hill."

Ruthie tilted her head. "South Hill, you say? Haven't heard from anyone there in quite some time. What brings you by?"

"We're helping the Chamber of Commerce dig into some of the town's old Christmas traditions," Hannah Leigh said. "One story keeps coming up. The dogwood tree and the love story that ended under it one snowy Christmas Eve."

Something flickered in Ruthie's eyes. "That old story?" she asked softly. "I hope you're not here to make fun of me."

"Not a chance, Ms. Danvers." Nate said.

"You may as well call me Ruthie if you're going to be all in my personal business. It's not a love story. There was no happy ending. It was a sad life story. A love that never earned its time."

"I'm sorry, Ms. Ruthie," Nate said. "We're just trying to understand what happened."

"We think we may have found a missing piece to that story." Hannah Leigh was so gentle with the old woman. He watched respectfully as the woman turned to her and softened.

Ruthie hesitated, then gestured toward the sofa. "Well, sit then. If we're talking about ghosts, might as well be comfortable."

"I understand you were a teacher," Hannah Leigh said.

"Yes. I taught my whole life."

She got the ball rolling. "Did you ever marry? Have children?"

"My life was abundant with love for every child I ever had the privilege to teach. I loved them all. Even the bratty ones, bless their hearts. Wasn't their fault." She touched her fingers to her lips. "I tracked their successes, mourned their failures, helped when I could. I never married or had children of my own."

"Because of Henry?"

She blinked. "It sounds ridiculous. You won't understand. Nobody does." She looked away. "You know when you've experienced the love of your life. I could never leave that behind. I still cling to that special time we spent together." Her eyes wandered to the side table.

Hannah Leigh caught Nate's attention, pointing to where Ruthie's attention had turned.

He noticed the ornate frame there. "Miss Danvers, is that a picture of you and Henry," he asked.

"It is."

Nate had stepped into plenty of homes over the years. Some gave off the vibe they'd soaked up decades of love, loss, and laughter and kept them all. In this little apartment, this whole woman's life fit neatly inside.

"Do you remember that night?" Hannah Leigh asked as they sat.

Ruthie nodded. "Every bit of it. Sometimes I forget what day it is, but I'll never forget him."

"Henry Bell must've been very special."

She nodded. "Sweet man, always carried a notebook and

a camera. Very smart, too. He was doing an important story for the paper about changes to the railroad that were affecting the east coast. He was in town over a month. We knew he'd have to leave eventually, but he got the news just before Christmas that his next assignment required that he leave right after Christmas. Neither of us wanted it to end."

"I guess it was harder right at the holidays."

"I think the hard part was that our feelings had grown so quickly. He was even spending time with my family. He'd show up at school with flowers. The children loved that. They'd tease he was my boyfriend." A grin brightened her face. "He was so much more than that."

"But he had to leave."

"I begged him to stay, but he couldn't. When my parents saw how upset I was, they forbade me to continue talking to him. My heart wouldn't allow it though. That's when we started leaving letters in the dogwood for each other. Every single day there were letters."

"Do you have the letters?"

She nodded. "Tied with a ribbon from the last gift he'd given me. I treasure everyone. He wrote beautiful letters." Pausing, she took in a tired breath. "He promised we'd be together. He asked me to meet him under the dogwood. Said he had something important we needed to discuss. But he never came."

"The snowstorm," Nate said.

Her voice wavered. "Yes. If you've never experienced thunder snow, it's a real thing. The thunder introduced snow so thick you couldn't see across the street, but I went to meet him. I waited as long as I could, but it was so cold, and so wet it was heavy. Even my eyelashes had ice in them. I tried to stay. I even sang *O Holy Night* to keep myself brave. Told myself if I could hum it three times through and he still hadn't shown, I'd go home."

Her eyes teared. "I made it all the way through. Three times. No Henry."

Nate's brows knit together. "Did you ever find out why he didn't show?"

"No, but I suppose he made something of himself in the city and just forgot about me and South Hill." She shrugged. "I suppose it was for the best. City life wasn't for me.

Silence settled between them, heavy and tender.

"You can trick a mind into forgetting, but not a heart. I let that part of mine stay buried under that tree." Ruthie looked down at her folded hands.

Hannah Leigh looked like she was swallowing back tears. "I'm so sorry."

"It's okay." Ruthie smiled gently. "I knew my one true love. I just wasn't his. Some people live a whole life and don't feel that."

Nate leaned forward, lowering his voice. "I don't think he meant to leave you, Ruthie."

She looked up sharply. "You don't have to say those things."

"I'm not." He shook his head. "I think something kept him from getting there. And I think we have proof of that."

"How?"

Hannah Leigh reached into her tote and placed the small gold locket in Ruthie's trembling hands. "We believe he was going to give this to you that night."

Ruthie gasped, brushing her thumb over the worn surface. "I've never seen this."

"Check the back," Hannah Leigh said.

Ruthie turned it over, eyes widening as she read the faint inscription aloud. "'I found my love under the dogwood. RD + HB. '" Her voice broke. "This was for me?"

"Those are your initials," Hannah Leigh pointed out. "Right?"

"We found it buried beneath the tree," Nate said. "We think it may have gotten covered up in that snowstorm, maybe he'd left it with one of his letters to you or something."

"It was there all this time?"

"We can't be sure. But it seems he never meant to miss that date." Hannah Leigh hitched a breath. "That locket is a fine gift, expensive in its day. We confirmed Harper's Jewelry in South Hill engraved the inscription. That's not just a Christmas present. It looks like a promise to me."

"I can't believe it. All these years…"

Ruthie clung to that locket, staring at his picture.

"The chain broke, and the dirt messed up the clasp a little. We'd like to take it back to Harper's Jewelry so they can clean it up for you. If you don't mind."

"I can't believe it's mine to keep. I hate for anyone to spend money on it. It's a keepsake no matter what the condition," she said.

"The Chamber of Commerce will foot the bill. Please allow us to do this for you. I can't promise how long it will take with the holidays and all, but if you can be patient, I think it would certainly be worth it. Plus, it would be in condition to wear."

"Oh my. Yes, I would love to wear it." A tear slid down her cheek. "Just knowing he'd meant to get that to me. That he didn't just leave me there. I've lived without the locket all these years, the information is most precious. I'd appreciate you getting it fixed."

"Then that's exactly what we'll do. Ruthie, it has been such a pleasure getting to meet you," Hannah Leigh said.

Nate couldn't take his eyes off the old woman, wondering how lonely she must get here with no family nearby. He raised a hand. "Pardon me, if I may, Ruthie, can I ask if you drive?"

"Oh no." She shook her head vehemently. "Haven't in years."

"I was wondering. Would you like us to take you to see the dogwood tree one day? It's beautiful, and you know it's the oldest dogwood in Virginia now. South Hill is pretty proud of it. Once the weather breaks, I'd love to take you on a tour of South Hill and to see the tree once again."

Her face seemed to brighten. "Really? I haven't been there in years. Why would you do that?"

"Why wouldn't we?" he said, hoping she'd accept the offer.

"And you can see where I found your locket!" Hannah Leigh's eyes brightened.

"Thank you for taking the time to bring this to me."
The locket opened with a soft click. She looked inside only a moment before shutting it again, her touch lingering, as if the memories might scatter if she let go too soon.

When Nate and Hannah Leigh stepped outside, the cold met them head-on, sharp enough to sting their cheeks. Neither spoke at first. The weight of Ruthie's story hung between them, fragile and aching.

He exhaled, watching his breath fog in the air. "Hard not to think about how long she's carried that kind of love."

Hannah Leigh nodded. "It's heartbreaking. All those years thinking she wasn't enough."

"She was," he said after a moment. "Maybe sometimes people simply run out of time."

"We're never guaranteed a tomorrow." She looked at him then, really looked, and something unspoken flickered in her eyes. He glanced away first, pretending to adjust his scarf.

"We should visit her again," she breathed. "Gloria mentioned she doesn't get many visitors."

"I was thinking the same thing. We will," he promised. "I think she'd like that."

They walked toward his truck, boots crunching on the frosted gravel. Hannah Leigh broke the silence. "Let's go harvest the *Love Left Behind* board and see what we can find about that other note. The one in block letters. I don't think it's connected to Ruthie, but something about it keeps bugging me."

Nate shot her a curious look. "Bugging you how?"

She hesitated, frowning a little. "I can't explain it. Just a feeling like whoever wrote it wasn't leaving a memory. They were trying to be found."

Back in South Hill, they were reading letters on the *Love Left Behind* board when Birdie appeared, wearing a Santa hat that had seen better days and clutching a bag of pralines to sell. "Well, don't y'all look like you've just seen the Ghost of Christmas Past," she said cheerfully. "If he's headed to the Colonial tonight, he'd better have tickets, because it's a sell-out!"

Nate let out a quick, amused huff. "We'll let him know."

Hannah Leigh nudged him. "Don't you go inviting ghosts."

He lifted his arms in another over-the-top ghostly shiver, the sound of her laugh exactly what he'd been aiming for.

Nate pulled into the lot beside her car and shifted into park. "Well," he said, glancing her way, "guess this is you."

"Guess so." She smiled, that tired-but-happy kind that always tugged at him.

He walked her to her car, watching her fumble for her keys. "You sure you're good to drive?"

"Promise." She opened the door, the cold air curling around them.

"Alright then." He hesitated, not wanting the night to end. "Goodnight, Hannah Leigh."

"Goodnight, Nate." She hurried toward the shop door, her determined stride as familiar as it was endearing.

He stood there a moment longer, hands in his pockets, before climbing back into his truck. He started the engine, but didn't pull out right away—just watched the light flick on inside as she disappeared through the door, and thought maybe heading home could wait a minute.

Ruthie's story had settled deep in him. It stuck with him.

Echoing like a song you thought you'd forgotten but somehow still knew every word to.

He parked on Main Street. The December air carried the faint scent of popcorn, where they were probably popping it by the bucketful to prepare for the movie tonight.

South Hill still carried a certain amount of small-town charm that he hoped would never change. He strolled down the street, taking the time to really look at all the decorations the merchants had worked so hard on. The judging would happen right after the Christmas tree lighting. Last year's People's Choice Winner was still his favorite though. It would be hard to beat. The local State Farm agency decorated a pole in sparkly garland, then tilted a kids' plastic ride-on car against it as if it had crashed. Sort of a playful public service announcement with a reminder not to let the pretty lights distract you.

Across the street, the lampposts glimmered under their garlands, each one part of the annual decorating contest. Stockings, grinches, and angels decorated the scene. In front of the fire station, they'd arranged a red fire hose into a Christmas tree shape, topped with the Company 7 South Hill Volunteer Fire Department logo.

These folks had really upped their game since last year. He couldn't help but grin as he passed Graham Hardware's entry. A wreath made from coiled extension cords and copper wire, above an artificial tree zip-tied to the lamppost that had paint brushes, tape measures and nuts and bolts all sparkling with glitter for ornaments. Half hardware, half-holiday magic.

Lundy Lane sponsored one lamppost too. Farmhouse

garland made entirely out of vintage flannel shirts. *Now that's clever.* He tugged on his own flannel collar with a quiet chuckle, thinking he could've donated a few old ones for the cause.

Harper's Jewelry trimmed the lamppost in front of their storefront in white and gold to match their display window which always shimmered with real gems and jewels. But for the holidays, a single velvet box with an heirloom ring shone beneath a halo of twinkle lights. Inside, a framed photo of Sandra and her granddaughter, Victoria, stood side by side wearing Santa hats. It reminded him what family legacy really looked like. Their lamppost was tastefully simple and elegant.

Victoria walked out just as he passed by.

"If there's any justice this Christmas," he murmured, "that lamppost's takin' home the blue ribbon."

Victoria waved, grinning. "It's not about winning, Coach. We just hope to out-sparkle them all!"

"In that case, mission accomplished." He gave her a thumbs up.

For a moment, he stood there, breathing in the town's life. The sound of the carolers warming up over in the pavilion, the faint jingle of the coffee shop bell, the sound of a train horn off in the distance. It was all so ordinary, and yet something about it felt like a reminder. That life, even in its quietest hours, had a way of circling back to unfinished business.

Later that night, sitting at his kitchen table, Nate spread out his notes and the photocopy of the letter they'd found in the post office. His laptop screen lit brightly against the dark, a half-empty mug of coffee cooling beside him.

Ruthie's words echoed in his head. *I sang O Holy Night three times.*

He couldn't shake that image. Something about that night, about Henry Bell not showing up, didn't sit right.

He dug deeper, emailing an old buddy who had the technical skills and access to search old archives that might result in something helpful. He hated waiting for answers he could almost see.

By midnight, his friend had come through, and Nate had three new pieces of the puzzle:

1. An article from the New York Times, confirming Henry Bell's byline and listing him as a staff reporter in 1964, and the clipping of the railroad story he'd been writing when he met Ruthie that ran on December 22nd.

2. A scan of an unclaimed personal effects list for Henry Bell from the La Crosse Hotel six-week stay in the registry dated December 27, 1964, including a receipt from Harper's Jewelry and some articles of clothing.

3. The Police Blotter recap printed the week of December 27 in the South Hill Enterprise 1964, noting the number of accidents during the storm, and one entry that had to be Henry Bell.

Nate continued to scan the police blotter recap until one held his attention. He blinked and re-read it twice.

Unidentified Man Found Near La Crosse Hotel: Early Sunday morning, Officer J.T. Collins responded to a call regarding an unconscious man discovered along the rail line behind the La Crosse Hotel. The man, believed to be in his early thirties, was suffering from exposure and transported by ambulance to Richmond General Hospital. He carried no identification, only a pocket notebook and a gold pen. Anyone with information is asked to contact the Sheriff's Office.

Nate sat back, the air in the room suddenly heavier. "Son of a gun," he murmured.

If Henry went to the hospital and then was sent home, this would at least prove he hadn't intentionally avoided meeting up with Ruthie that night. Nate rubbed a hand over his jaw, the realization hitting hard. Ruthie had waited under the dogwood, believing he'd left her behind.

But Henry had tried to keep his promise.

He opened his phone and typed a message before he could overthink it:

NATE: Got some new dots worth connecting. Meet tomorrow after cookie judging?

Within seconds, his screen lit up. Tension eased in him just enough for a grin.

Outside, South Hill glittered under the winter sky, the lamppost lights reflecting off snow-dusted roofs. From the outside, it looked like any other small town in December. Peaceful, and picture-perfect.

But under all that sparkle, Nate knew better. This town was full of tangled cords, half-buried secrets, and the kind of hope that refused to die quietly.

CHAPTER SEVENTEEN

The next morning, Hannah Leigh had one hand on her phone opening her calendar app and the other wrapped around a Bringleton's mega cocoa. Her nerves as frayed as the bow hanging from the Chamber's office wreath. Underneath all of South Hill's holiday sparkle, things weren't adding up.

The visit with Ruthie the day before was still rattling around in her head like a sleigh bell without a clacker. And then there was that block letter note.

When she stepped back into the office and spotted Birdie perched there like a holiday-themed gargoyle, the present rolled in. Birdie was having way too much fun with all of this, and that made Hannah Leigh half-wonder if the old bird may have written the note.

"I brought pralines." Birdie offered a tin shaped like Santa's sleigh.

"That's the reason you came by?"

"I was across the way when I saw your aunt's car." She scrounged around in her purse. "Oh! And look what I found in my attic." She pulled out an old, yellowed newspaper clipping. The photo was blurry, but unmistakably Ruthie Danvers. She had to have been in her twenties, standing under the dogwood tree with a man who looked suspiciously like Henry Bell. The story described a family welcoming an out-of-towner at Thanksgiving. Apparently, Henry Bell spent the holiday with the Danvers family.

"Where did you get this?" Hannah Leigh asked.

"Like I said. My attic. My daddy saved every newspaper he ever touched. Didn't throw out a scrap of anything except his back. I had this moment where I figured I should research the papers around that time. It was Thanksgiving week that ran." Birdie shrugged. "Sometimes the past begs to be seen."

With that, Birdie floated out, leaving a sugary trail of pecans and scandal.

Aunt Winnie walked up behind Hannah Leigh and peered at the photo. "Well. That Birdie is a pot-stirrer if I've ever seen one."

"Christmas miracles come wrapped in the truth sometimes, I guess."

Later that evening, Hannah Leigh sat in her room at Aunt Winnie's, staring at the photo. There was no doubt the man was Henry. The recent note on the board didn't seem to go with that story.

Either way, Nate was right. They were waist-deep in peppermint bark and secrets. They'd be judging cookies this afternoon and chasing ghosts in their spare time. She just hoped the two didn't collide.

Hannah Leigh's phone hadn't stopped pinging from updates about the Hometown Holiday Festival. Getting down to the wire, Aunt Winnie showed up with a rolling suitcase, a shopping bag full of ribbon, and enough holiday spirit to power the courthouse lights.

Hannah Leigh had barely made it back to the Chamber office after a whirlwind cookie-judging dash — she'd had to run in, sample, score, and dash back out — leaving Nate and the others to tally the votes and announce the winners. She was still catching her breath when Aunt Winnie bustled in, arms loaded with shopping bags she plopped right onto the desk.

"What's all this for?" Hannah Leigh asked, eyeing the pile.

"Sunday's wrap up," Aunt Winnie said. "I have gifts for the volunteers. I need you to help me wrap them."

"Happy to do that for you. What are they?"

Aunt Winnie unzipped the suitcase and handed her a box. "This one is for you. You don't have to wrap your own," she said.

"Thank you." Hannah Leigh slipped her finger under the tab and opened the gift. Inside, a small jar of chutney in a mason jar with an embroidered snowflake design on buffalo-check flannel fabric.

"Thank you. I love it, Aunt Winnie. Did you do the embroidery, too?"

"I most certainly did. The best gifts are homemade. My volunteers, and you, my dear, deserve my best."

"Everyone will love them." Before Hannah Leigh could finish, the bell on the front door jingled. Birdie appeared as if summoned, holding a shoebox and a yearbook. It looked like someone had rescued the yearbook from a trunk in the church basement.

"I've got something for you, girls." She plopped the box onto the table and flipped open the yearbook to a page she'd dog-eared with a sprig of mistletoe.

"Margaret Jane Russell," she announced. "I bet that's the woman who wrote that note on the *Love Left Behind* board." Birdie flipped open the yearbook and poked her finger at a pretty brunette's face.

Hannah Leigh leaned closer. "I can see her in that picture. But how does that prove she wrote the note?"

"She and Clarence were smitten back in the day. Everyone in school thought they'd get married. Then her family moved away. It was all rather sudden. Why else would she show up here after all these years and buy one of those condos? She's right back where she fell in love with him. I'm telling you. It's love coming full circle." Birdie clutched her hands to her chest.

"Birdie, that is a wonderfully romantic tale, but it doesn't prove a thing."

"It explains why Clarence is acting like a party pooper, and if the locket isn't connected to him after all, I'd bet my reputation it has something to do with Margaret Jane and that dogwood," Birdie said. "Call Margaret Jane and ask if she wrote the note." She shoved the phone number toward Winnie.

Aunt Winnie lifted a brow. "Does she know we're calling?"

Birdie shrugged. "Not yet. But she will once this one here dials." She waved her arthritic finger toward Hannah Leigh. "I'll tell you the number."

Hannah Leigh opened her phone, heart fluttering. "What

do I even say?"

"Say Christmas brought you back around to a mystery, and her name lit the path. Dial 555-1166." Birdie winked and waved herself out, pralines trailing behind like a sugar-dusted sleigh.

As the front door closed, Hannah Leigh sat back hoping Margaret Jane wouldn't answer, and thank goodness her wish came true. It went to voice mail.

Just then, her phone lit up again. This time a message from Nate.

NATE: Everything okay? Want to grab cocoa later?

She smiled, thumb hovering over the screen.

HANNAH LEIGH: Would love that. Meet you after I finish at the Chamber?

Three dots danced for a second.

NATE: Oops...rain check? I need to run over to Colonial for an electrical 911.

She stared at the message a moment longer than she meant to, then nodded to no one and slipped the phone away. Still, the small sag of her shoulders betrayed what her heart already knew—disappointment liked to pretend it didn't hurt.

She glanced again at Margaret Jane's photo wondering if she and the mayor had been lighthearted and in love. If her coming back had anything to do with it, or the mayor's mood.

It was hard to picture the cranky mayor in love like that. If that's why Margaret Jane moved back, you'd think that fantasy would've blown up when she saw his moody scowl he seemed to wear all the time.

Eventually the pieces would fall into place like ornaments on a tree waiting for the star on top.

CHAPTER EIGHTEEN

By Thursday afternoon, the day before the festival kicks off, it was all hands on deck. Hannah Leigh was juggling more Christmas chaos than cocoa mugs to be sold at the Christmas Craft Market. Cookie contest entries doubled overnight, the drooping garland was demanding an immediate fixing, and a choir director losing her voice had her knee-deep in merry mayhem.

The *Hometown Holiday Festival* was barreling toward them faster than Santa on a caffeine buzz, and Aunt Winnie was in her element. Clipboards, duct tape, and pure determination. She'd turn this town into a winter wonderland if it meant gluing the garland on herself.

The countdown was ticking, and the day was flying by. It would be a miracle if they finished everything by morning.

Hannah Leigh needed a break, so she slipped out the back door of the Chamber of Commerce. She headed straight to the coffee shop even though her conscience was thumping louder than reindeer hooves on a rooftop which was giving her a headache.

Inside Bringleton's, roasted espresso and vanilla comforted her. She spotted Nate at a corner table, sipping hot cocoa and flipping through a book.

Is it being back in South Hill, or spending time with Nate, that feels so good about this visit?

The thought hung there for a heartbeat. She took in a breath and walked over, pretty sure Nate was the answer. "How are you doing?"

"Good," Nate said, clearing his things from the table across from him. "Join me."

But just as Hannah Leigh pulled the chair out, her phone buzzed.

WINNIE: Mayor's tree lighting dry-run in 15 minutes. Need you there ASAP.

"That would've been so nice." She groaned. "I can't." She flipped her phone around so he could see the message. "I've been summoned."

"Sorry." Nate looked disappointed. "Maybe we can get together later. Dinner?"

"I'll text you. Before this, my day was packed, but somehow this little temporary assignment keeps growing.

"You're already waist high in this thing," he teased. "No turning back now."

She pushed her hair behind her ear. "It might drown me before it's all said and done."

"Hope not, and you've got to eat. Keep me on speed dial. And here, take this." Nate pressed a small, red-wrapped box into her hand. "For later."

The little gift took her by surprise. "What did you do?"

"Just a little something. I was thinking about you and how busy you've been. Go on. They are waiting on you."

"Yeah. Thanks." She spun and rushed toward the door. Before she reached the tree-lighting area, she took a moment to open the little box. A Bringleton's gift card and a paper ornament that read,

For when the day runs long, and the town runs wild.
Your cocoa is on me.
Conversation optional, but I'm hoping for both.
        —Nate

She hugged the card before tucking it into her coat pocket. The sweet gesture made it impossible to hide her excitement. *He like-likes me. Like really likes me.* She couldn't stop smiling if she tried.

And with that, the rush to help with the tree lighting dry run didn't seem as bad. In fact, she didn't even dread dealing with the grumpy mayor.

By the time Hannah Leigh reached the square, the half-strung garland and ladders leaning every which way in the middle of decorating the jumbo Christmas tree looked nothing less than chaotic.

Aunt Winnie stood at the center of it all like a five-foot-tall field marshal, clipboard in one hand, cocoa in the other. "Places, people!" she called. "Christmas Craft Market is the opener for South Hill Hometown Holiday Festival, and this tree needs to shine like it's guiding shepherds tomorrow night."

Hannah Leigh jogged up, breath puffing white. "How's it going?"

"Depends on who you ask," Winnie said. "Here comes South Hill's notoriously grumpy mayor now. He's the one who insisted on a dry run. It's flipping a switch. He's done it the last three years. Why does he need practice? It's throwing my whole plan off."

"It'll be okay. Let's just get through it and give him peace of mind," she reassured her aunt. "I'll handle it."

The mayor stomped toward them, his scarf trailing behind him like a battle flag. Mayor Clarence Collier stood near the base of the tree, clipboard in one hand, disapproval in the other. "Winnie, this whole spectacle's gotten out of hand," he barked. "Do we really need synchronized lights *and* a countdown? Folks just want to see the tree, drink their cocoa, and go home."

Winnie smiled sweetly. "Clarence, the people of South Hill want wonder. And this year, they're getting it, even if I have to staple it to the lampposts myself."

He grumbled about budgets and power bills. "And the *Enterprise* is sending someone over? Last thing I need is another newspaper headline making me look like Santa's disgruntled intern."

From the risers, Margaret Jane looked up from a box of hymn books. "Then maybe try smiling, Clarence. Cameras like that."

For a moment his scowl cracked, something warm flickering behind it, then he cleared his throat. "We'll see."

"Margaret Jane!" Winnie bustled over. "You're an answer to prayer. Darlene lost her voice yelling at her grandkids, and we need an alto for the choir."

Margaret Jane strolled up, scarf bright as holly berries, volunteering before anyone could stop her. "I'd love to help with the choir," she said sweetly, earning a grunt from Clarence that might've been a yes.

But when Margaret Jane and the mayor's eyes locked, she blanched.

"Are you okay?" Hannah Leigh reached to steady her. "You look like you might faint."

"I might," she whispered. "I swear I just went back in time to the first time he ever looked into my eyes like that." She blinked twice slowly. "No, I'm okay. I can do this."

"Perfect. Breathe, honey. Can't have you falling out in the middle of a Christmas carol." Winnie turned back to the crowd. "Join the choir in the gazebo. Rehearsal and then cookies and cocoa. Thank you so much. You're saving the day."

Margaret Jane practically jogged off to get to the choir.

"Saved the day? Aunt Winnie, you are putting entirely too much pressure on everyone. This is supposed to be fun."

"It is fun. I'm making sure of it. And did you see the way Clarence and Margaret Jane looked at each other?" She pulled a whistle from her pocket and gave it a two-toot coaches tweet, then hollered, "Volunteers? Get a vendor map over here, and enough crime scene tape to mark off your spots. Chop, chop."

"Goodness gracious. Crime scene tape?" Hannah Leigh said.

"It was free. Can't say no to free," Aunt Winnie said. "Trust me. I've got this. This ain't my first rodeo. Well, it would be my first rodeo, but it's not my first Christmas event."

"I get it. Okay, don't let me interfere." Hannah Leigh took a step back. Trying with all her might to stay out of it and keep her opinions to herself.

The volunteers scattered. Then Aunt Winnie walked over and whispered to Hannah Leigh, "Did you know once upon a time the mayor was so gaga over Margaret Jane that when she left town, he lost his joy, and his sense of humor right along with it. He wasn't always this cranky, you know."

"Aunt Winnie, did you arrange this tree lighting practice and being short one choir singer to force them into proximity?"

"Looks like Christmas magic to me?" Aunt Winnie tried to look innocent, but Hannah Leigh wasn't buying it.

"The kind you pin to the lamp post yourself? Shame on you. Don't you have enough on your plate without becoming South Hill's Cupid on the Corner, too?"

"Cupid on the Corner? I like that. I might use that for Valentine's Day." Aunt Winnie scribbled a note on her clipboard. "It'll be fine. Don't you worry about me."

"I'm worried more about the mayor and Margaret Jane than you at the moment."

She swatted Hannah Leigh's arm. "We're family. You stop that. Believe me. Those two will thank me if I can get them to stop musing from a distance now that she's back, and get on with falling in love for real."

Hannah Leigh followed her gaze to where Clarence was pretending to fuss with the power cord, sneaking glances toward the music. "Maybe that *is* a possibility."

Winnie's smile had the type of warmth you can't plug in. "Oh, honey, around here, Christmas has a way of mending things."

I wonder if South Hill Christmas magic applies to visitors, too? A girl can dream.

At the top of the hour, Hannah Leigh guided the mayor through the tree-lighting cues and helped hang glittering stars from lampposts. Then, she double-checked the signage on the vendor spaces and the official Christmas Craft Market map.

At the last minute, a vendor from North Carolina had to back out because of a family emergency, leaving one empty booth. Aunt Winnie was going to have a fit over that.

Or maybe not. Did she even need to know? That's when Hannah Leigh had the bright idea of leaving the space already assigned to them to use herself. She could make another *Love Left Behind* Board to set up in that space.

No one missed the South Hill Christmas Craft Market. They sourced the best one-of-a-kind crafts, baked goods, and gift ideas around. Plus, in yesterday's meeting, they confirmed the senior center was offering a round-trip bus to and from the community center every hour. That was the precise demographic that could help her solve this locket mystery.

Plus, projections for attendance at the South Hill Hometown Holiday Festival were about four times the usual. This was her best chance to uncover a lead.

After she completed everything on her to-do list, she returned to the Chamber of Commerce and raided the storage closet. *Jackpot!* An old classroom-sized bulletin board, velvet ribbon, and twinkle lights did the trick. Then she used the fancy plotter printer to create the sign.

Love Left Behind Board
Have a memory to mend? Share your lost love story here.

The next morning marked the start of South Hill's Hometown Holiday Festival — Day One, the Christmas Craft Market — the official launch into two solid weeks of twinkle lights, cocoa stands, and small-town cheer that would carry straight through Christmas Day. By evening, the tree lighting would flip the switch on the whole town, every storefront and lamppost glowing like a postcard.

It was a big day and just the first in the two-week frenzy of holiday cheer that Aunt Winnie was heading up. Hannah Leigh was caffeinated and ready.

She arrived early, bundled and hopeful, to set up her booth. She propped up the huge *Love Left Behind* board, smoothing its edges and whispering a silent prayer that folks would stop long enough to share a memory, a name, or maybe a clue.

Then, she picked up her radio, an ear mic, and updated clipboard at the Chamber office, and was ready to roll. Her job was helping Aunt Winnie make sure the only hitch in the day was the one pulling Santa down Main Street, tossing candy canes at noon.

Residents must've flocked to the secondary *Love Left Behind* board faster than to the kettle corn booth, pinning hand-written notes and anonymous confessions like snowflakes. Each was different. Some were funny; others wistful. But one made Hannah Leigh freeze in place.

He never showed.

I waited under the dogwood, red coat, white mittens.

Snow fell. So did my heart.

She stared at that one for a long time. The words pulling something deep inside her. An ache she knew too well. Hope giving way to disappointment. Promise turning quiet.

Nate came up behind her with a candy cane tucked behind his ear like he'd forgotten it was there. "What's up?"

"I thought this board might tease out some ideas." She nodded toward a note in shaky block print written in red marker. "But look at this letter. It matches everything Birdie said, but we know Ruthie didn't write it."

Nate's brow furrowed as he leaned in to read it. "He never showed. Red coat, white mittens... it's almost like the same story told twice."

Nate pulled his phone from his pocket and snapped a photo. "Now we've got it. Put it back on the board before Birdie accuses us of tampering with evidence." He slid the phone away, grinning. "Come on. You need a break from all this sleuthing. How about I win you a snow globe at the Snowball Toss booth?"

Her mouth curved. "Are you trying to woo me, Nate Collier?"

"Trying? I was hoping I already had a decent start."

He took her hand, warm and steady, and led her toward the far side of the festival grounds where laughter and music filled the air. Children lined up to toss foam "snowballs" at painted targets, giggling when bells rang out from successful hits.

"While we're waiting for me to impress you with my skills, I've been dying to talk to you about some things I found out about our Henry Bell."

"What? When?"

"For a couple days now. Every time we tried to connect one of us was too busy. But here's what I wanted to share. I asked a friend to do some digging for me on Henry, and he found a few interesting things." Nate walked her through each of the findings from the newspaper articles, all the way to the police blotter notes.

"Oh my gosh! Do you think he died that night?"

"No. I searched the local obituaries for that time and didn't come up with anything, but my friend is still trying to chase a couple of leads. I've got all the documents printed out. At least we can share that much with Ruthie."

"This is great," she said. "More than I could've hoped for."

"No." Nate gave her a nod and then stepped up to the snowball game, paid his ticket, and fired off three perfect throws in a row. "That's what you call great."

She jumped up and hugged him. "That is great."

Nate held on to her an extra second until the attendant handed him a glittering snow globe with a miniature dogwood tree inside. Nate held it out like a trophy. "Told you I could win you one."

She shook her head. "Show-off."

"It's for you," he said, but as she reached for it, something over his shoulder made her pause. The smile faded from her lips.

"What is it?" he asked, turning slightly.

Hannah Leigh pointed back toward the courtyard. A few townspeople gathered around the Love Left Behind Board, whispering. Among them stood the mayor, arms crossed tight, frown etched deep as he stared at the notes.

Nate followed her gaze. "Are you looking at Uncle Clarence? Does he—"

"Yeah," she whispered. "He looks like a man who just read something he wishes he hadn't."

CHAPTER NINETEEN

Hannah Leigh was now convinced that South Hill had invented its own definition of the word "busy."

It wasn't just full calendars or long lists of chores. Busy in South Hill during December was a kind of glittering, jingle-belled, praline-scented whirlwind that never slowed down.

By the time Saturday dawned, Hannah Leigh had already sprinted across the town square twice. Once to check on the cookie contest table and once to referee an argument between the brass band and the carolers about who got the prime spot outside Bringleton's. Both sides claimed tradition, and both had Birdie whispering in their ears like an ornamented devil on each shoulder.

Now, standing in the middle of Main Street with her scarf trailing and her phone buzzing in her coat pocket, Hannah Leigh felt like the whole town was holding its breath before the curtain rose on opening day of the Hometown Holiday Festival.

And if something went wrong, all fingers would point at her, and she couldn't let Aunt Winnie down like that.

Across the way, the craft tent was already humming when she ducked inside. The air was thick with the smell of glue sticks and cinnamon, children's giggles bubbling like sleigh bells as they clutched paintbrushes and glitter shakers. At least a dozen kids crowded around long tables, turning paper plates into reindeer masks and pinecones into glittery little angels with crooked halos.

"About time you showed," Nate called from the far end. Rolled sleeves, sawdust still clinging to his boots, he looked like he'd stepped straight off a project site into Santa's workshop.

Hannah Leigh pushed her hair off her face. "Don't start. I've been putting out tinsel fires all morning."

"Literal fires?" He arched a brow.

She shot him a look. "Yes. Someone's hot glue gun melted a pile of garland."

Nate chuckled, low and warm, and handed her a pair of scissors. "I can see the headline now. South Hill fires Christmas."

"Don't tempt fate," she said, sliding into place beside him. "Thanks for coming to help." Their arms brushed as they leaned over the same pile of construction paper, and for a second, the room felt smaller. Warmer.

He passed her a mason jar of glitter. "Here. Supervise. I'll wrangle the paint."

She lifted the jar. "Supervise? Have you seen what happens when I supervise? Glitter ends up in people's hair for weeks."

"That's half the point."

They worked on crafts until the top of the hour when parents began showing up to whisk the kids off to the next thing.

"I think our work here is done," she said. "That went pretty well."

"Guess we make a good team." Nate swept glitter from her sleeve.

"Except for the glitter tattoo," she teased, lifting her forearm to show off a line of glitter. "I warned you I'm glitter intolerant."

"I kind of like the way you sparkle." His words unhurried. "Either way, we're leaving a trail."

Hannah Leigh glanced toward the tent flap as jingling bells drifted in on a cool breeze. "Speaking of trails, I hear the horses clopping down the street. Come on."

Outside the tent, sleigh bells jingled in a steady rhythm. Hannah Leigh peeked out and smiled at the sight of two draft horses pulling a sled piled with families bundled in quilts, their breath puffing white clouds into the air. The driver, old Mr. Hollis, tipped his cap as the sled clopped past.

The sound of the horses mixed with the choir warming up on the courthouse steps. A few notes of *O Come, All Ye Faithful* carried on the cold air, sweet and shaky, while the brass band tuned up across the street, trumpets buzzing. Over it all rose Birdie's voice from somewhere in the crowd, narrating like she was the official festival announcer.

"Bless her heart," Hannah Leigh muttered. "I bet Aunt Winnie wishes she could lock Birdie up until this festival is over."

"We all complain about her, but I think folks will actually miss her if she ever stopped," said Nate.

Hannah Leigh glanced at him, smiling despite her exhaustion. "You really think so?"

"Sure. Without Birdie, this town would be pretty boring."

She couldn't argue with that.

Nate leaned down beside her, close enough that she caught the clean scent of cedar and pine clinging to his jacket. "You're good at this," he said.

She kept her eyes focused on the horses going down the street, hoping to hide the sudden flush rising in her cheeks. "Bossing people around?"

"Making chaos feel like Christmas."

Her throat skipped at the unexpected compliment. She wanted to thank him again for helping. To tell him the way he steadied the kids, and steadied her, felt like more than coincidence. But before she could, Birdie's voice split through the tent like a trumpet.

"Best news ever!" Birdie bustled over in a blur of red sequins on a Mrs. Santa coat flashing like a disco ball. "Margaret Jane agreed to meet Hannah Leigh!"

Hannah Leigh blinked at her. "What are you talking about?"

Birdie grinned like the cat who'd stolen Santa's cookies. "Margaret Jane Russell herself. Said she's ready to talk about the dogwood and that locket. I may have nudged her with a praline bribe, but she's expecting you."

Nate's head snapped toward Hannah Leigh, his expression unreadable but his eyes sparking with both caution and curiosity.

"Birdie—" Hannah Leigh started, but Aunt Winnie interrupted her when she strode over like the conquering general of Christmas, her apron dusted with powdered sugar and a tray of pralines held high.

"We did it!" she announced. "Minnie Pearl's Pralines are

officially back in South Hill. And judging by the crowd at the booth, they're already a hit. Here." She pressed the tray forward toward them. "Have one. I'm passing out samples."

Hannah Leigh snagged a sugared pecan and bit in, the buttery crunch melting on her tongue.

"Now that," Nate said, chewing thoughtfully, "is Christmas."

Aunt Winnie winked. "See! This recipe has the power to mend broken hearts. Or at least bribe a few gossip queens into cooperation." Then she swung around the corner, cheerfully shouting "Praline samples," into the afternoon.

Beside her, Nate shifted closer. Their shoulders brushed again, and this time neither moved away. "I think she's talking about Birdie," Hannah Leigh teased.

"You know she is. Hey, did I tell you that I'm impressed by how you're keeping all these old gals reined in?"

"Thanks. I needed to hear that today."

His gaze lingered a heartbeat too long, steady and warm. Then a crash of sleigh bells around the corner broke the spell.

She sighed. "Duty calls."

"I'm coming too." The two of them zipped around the corner to see Aunt Winnie trying to help untangle the sleigh reins while the driver, old Mr. Hollis, shouted apologies and the horses jingled like they were auditioning for a Christmas album.

"Aunt Winnie! Are you okay?"

"Nothing to see here! The horses just got spooked by the smell of the pralines," Aunt Winnie said, patting one horse's nose. "Can't say I blame 'em. These could stir up anybody's sweet tooth."

Hannah Leigh breathed a sigh of relief, and Nate ran over to help Mr. Hollis.

The rest of the afternoon was a blur. Hannah Leigh still divvied her time hustling between events, the cookie contest where one tray of snowman cookies had suspiciously turned into reindeer heads. The wreath judging nearly came to blows when the judges couldn't agree on how to score bow placement, and the sled rides ran long because every child in town begged for one more loop.

Everywhere she turned, Nate was there. Handing her a mug of cocoa. Holding a ladder steady while she adjusted twinkle lights. Grinning when Birdie announced to anyone within earshot that "romance was brewing faster than a kettle of cider."

By dusk, Hannah Leigh's legs ached, her hair smelled of pine and pralines, and her phone buzzed with more reminders than she could handle. But when she paused at the edge of the square and saw the town lit up like a thousand memories stitched together, she felt a lump in her throat.

This was South Hill. Sparkling. Messy. Hopeful.

And right in the middle of it, Nate Collier.

Back inside the tent, Aunt Winnie packed up the last pralines, Birdie hummed off-key carols while sweeping sequins, and Nate carried a stack of leftover craft supplies toward the door.

Hannah Leigh reached for her coat, but her gaze lingered on Birdie's text.

BIRDIE: *Margaret Jane agreed to meet.*

The locket. The tree. The secrets.

For all the cocoa tubs and carols, for all the sugar and sleigh rides, there was a romantic mystery waiting just beneath the sparkle, and her lonely heart couldn't wait to hear about it.

And Hannah Leigh also knew, deep down, that tonight's festival frenzy was only the beginning.

CHAPTER TWENTY

Hannah Leigh felt a knot of anxiety tighten in her stomach as she approached the door.

A fresh pine wreath hung on the door of Margaret Jane's condo. Beside her, Aunt Winnie tightened the red ribbon on a tin of pralines.

"You ready, honey?"

"As I'll ever be." Hannah Leigh tugged her scarf loose and knocked.

The door opened. Margaret Jane, wearing a red, buttoned cardigan with a pretty silver angel brooch. Her blue eyes carried the calm of someone who'd weathered plenty.

"Come on in," Margaret Jane said, warm but careful. "No sense catching a cold."

The living room was tidy, almost too tidy, like one of those Airbnbs that are sparse and void of anything personal. Only one picture graced the mantel. A young woman wearing a plaid dress, smiling beneath the Colonial sign.

Winnie set the pralines on the table. "A little thank you for jumping in and helping with the choir, and for that lovely solo."

Margaret Jane tugged on the ribbon and opened the tin. "They look delicious. Thank you. Have a seat."

Hannah Leigh sat down and then waited a beat before reaching inside her coat pocket and setting the oval locket in front of Margaret Jane. It was risky to pretend they didn't know who the locket belonged to, but it was the best way to shake out the intertwined stories. "I found this locket near the old dogwood. Do you recognize the people in the photographs inside?"

A faint breath caught. She turned it over with a trembling hand, tracing the faint engraving. "So beautiful," she whispered, opening it. "But no, I don't know these people."

Hannah Leigh hesitated. "Someone said you might have had some history with that tree. A love story?"

"I definitely have a story," she smiled, bittersweet. "But it's mine, not theirs." She folded her hands, gazing past them out the window. "I was eighteen. He was twenty. We thought we had forever figured out. We didn't."

"Don't we all think we have all the answers at that age?" Aunt Winnie teased.

"First met under that dogwood. Me reading, him chasing an overthrown ball. Years later we found each other again at the train station. My father had passed, and somehow he filled that quiet. We were inseparable for weeks while I helped settle the estate."

"Young love always feels like destiny," Winnie said as if she'd lived that too.

"Until it doesn't." A wistful laugh had her shaking her head. "His family didn't approve. That Christmas he asked if I'd meet him under the dogwood. He wanted to elope. We'd figure out the rest later."

Winnie leaned forward, elbows on knees. "Elope?" Her voice filled with interest.

Hannah Leigh could imagine a proposal under that tree.

"I was so excited. Everyone knows the story of the lovers who were supposed to meet under the dogwood. I'd dreamed of being the one who actually got to find their true love there. But I couldn't run off and get married without telling Momma. Only when I told her she became outraged. She packed us up and hauled me to Delaware that night. By spring, I tried to check on things back here only to find he'd married someone else."

The room went still.

Hannah Leigh leaned in, her voice low. "Someone thought maybe you were the one who wrote this note on the *Love Left Behind* board." She read it. "A man beneath the dogwood. A broken heart. A promise unkept."

"I did." Her smile wavered. "He was the most romantic man I ever knew. He still holds that title in my heart. But life went on. I married and had a good life. Still, I wonder what might've been. I guess I just couldn't resist putting that note on the board."

Winnie reached over and squeezed her hand. "You really loved him."

"More than anything, I still wish him peace." Margaret Jane crossed the room to a cedar chest, pulling out a folded church-social bulletin, a ribbon and an old photograph of herself with a tall young man. "That was Clarence," she said with affection still hanging on the words.

Winnie blinked. "Clarence Collier?"

Margaret Jane nodded. "We were careful. He came from folks who thought little of mine. We were in a different class, but I never felt like he was ashamed of me. But he married so quickly that I have to wonder if it was ever real."

The words landed like a church door closing. Not loud. Just final.

Margaret Jane straightened and managed a smile. "Christmas has a way of stirring settled things. Sometimes that hurts."

"Then maybe it's time for some healing," said Hannah Leigh. She put the locket back in her pocket.

Winnie stood, eyes glistening. "Thank you for trusting us with your story. We won't breathe a word. But you've probably figured out Birdie was the 'someone' we mentioned. She's got a knack for spreading news faster than a grassfire." Winnie smiled. "Still, she's good people. Tell her straight it's private, and she'll button up tight."

Margaret Jane gave a small nod. "Noted."

They lingered a few more minutes, as women do when they have already said the hardest words. Then came the hugs, soft goodbyes, and the slow shuffle toward the door.

Outside, twilight painted the sky a pale lavender. A cardinal lit on a low branch near the porch, a flicker of red against the quiet.

At the car, Hannah Leigh looked back. Margaret Jane stood framed in the window, one hand resting on the sill. A woman who had learned how to keep living with what she'd lost.

As Hannah Leigh got into the car, a quiet thought settled in her heart. Maybe some loves didn't end at all; they just waited for the right moment to be found again.

CHAPTER TWENTY-ONE

Hannah Leigh and Aunt Winnie climbed into the SUV, shivering while the heater coughed to life. "This is when I wish I drove one of those little cars that heats in thirty seconds." Hannah Leigh rubbed her hands briskly together.

"Head straight to Bringleton's," Aunt Winnie said, blowing into her palms. "I need something hot enough to thaw me clear down to my toes."

And she did just that. Hannah Leigh hopped out of the car, jogged inside and came back a few minutes later with two steaming cups. "One cocoa, extra marshmallows, the way you like it."

Aunt Winnie wrapped her hands around the cup and pressed it to her cheek. "Lordy goodness, I could climb right inside this."

They sat for a moment, the hum of the heater and the carols on the radio softening the air between them.

"Clarence," Aunt Winnie said finally. "I can't believe the person Margaret Jane described is the same Clarence as our mayor. It's mind boggling."

Hannah Leigh turned the locket in her pocket, feeling the cool metal slide against her fingertips. "One and the same."

"It's hard for me to think of that man as romantic," Aunt Winnie said. "But he's carried something heavy. You can see it in the way he stands when people cheer too loud. Like he doesn't know how to accept joy. His daddy was a hard man to please. And losing Elaine near broke him. Still, choices are choices."

Outside, the square shimmered in evening light. A couple stopped by the *Love Left Behind* board to pin a note. Across the way, Birdie popped up near the nativity scene as if conjured from thin air, then darted off toward Harper's Jewelry, a ribbon of news trailing in her wake. *Silent Night* floated through the air, soft and sure.

Hannah Leigh thumbed her phone and typed:

HANNAH LEIGH: Found answers. Found more questions. Can you meet?

The typing dots appeared, paused, then:

NATE: Give me twenty. Fixing lights before the tree lighting.

Her mouth lifted into a smile. "I'm going to meet Nate."

"You should. Go." Aunt Winnie shooed her with a mittened hand. "I'll bring the rest of this cocoa to the Chamber and bully the mayor into tasting the pralines again. He needs sugar if he's going to admit hard things. He knows Margaret Jane is back. There's no way he didn't recognize her when she came right out and told him she should smile for the camera. He's just playing coy."

"Or hiding from the truth. I agree." Hannah Leigh hugged her. "Thank you."

"For what?"

"For being you."

"Always." Aunt Winnie's smile made her look lit from

the inside. "Now drop me off at the office so you can scoot."

The whole town hummed with holiday activities as Hannah Leigh zipped back across town where Nate was stringing the last row of lights on the huge town tree. He climbed down the ladder, brushing off his hands. "You good?"

"Better," she said, and told him everything. The living room that smelled like cinnamon, the cardinal sparking red when they left, the ribbon and the program, the way Margaret Jane's voice had trembled when she spoke of her lost love.

He whistled. "Love can be messy. And confusing."

"Yeah," she said. "When you find the right one, hang on tight."

He nudged a coil of wire with his boot. "Did any of it have to do with the dogwood?"

"It did. The man she said was the most romantic and handsome she'd ever known, the one she waited for, is someone you know very well."

He arched a brow. "Not me, I hope. She's way too old for me."

"It's your uncle," she said.

Nate froze. "What?" He let out a breath, half disbelief, half resignation. "You know, I can see it. He and Elaine had an odd marriage. Very formal. So, Margaret Jane being back must be what's got him winding tighter in the cranky department than normal. Guess that explains it."

"I think so," Hannah Leigh said. "I promised not to share her side. Still, them both pretending not to notice each other is crazy. I just want the truth to stop running."

"Then let's invite the truth to them." Nate reached into his jacket pocket to pull out a small envelope. "If anyone can make that happen it's you. You're the best woman I've ever met. I made you something. Nothing fancy. Just something to help you keep confident in that bravery I so admire."

"What?" She opened it carefully. A coin-sized hand carved wooden dogwood blossom lay inside, simple and sure. The words *'Work your magic'* written in Sharpie around the edge. The woodgrain raised like quiet words under her fingers. "It's beautiful," she said. "Did you make it?"

"I did. Carved it out of some maple I had in my workshop. I was thinking about you."

"It's perfect. I'll keep it in my pocket so when I need it I've got it. Thank you."

He nodded toward the tent where the mayor worked on his speech. "He's in there, writing talking points for the ceremony. We could wait till morning, but I know him. He sleeps worse with secrets than with truths he didn't plan for."

She looked toward the tent, then back at Nate. "Let's do it now. No fuss. Just let him know Margaret Jane's here. He can't pretend he doesn't know then. After that, it's his move."

Nate smiled, that steady, quiet kind that always settled her nerves. "I'm with you."

They walked over to the makeshift festival office which was really just a small wall tent with a little ceramic heater fighting to warm the air.

Inside, a single lamp that cast a soft circle across the desk. Papers stacked in careful piles next to a cup of coffee.

Clarence looked up as they entered, his posture stiffening. "Evening," he said. "Getting ready for the tree lighting. I hate speeches."

"You've done a hundred of them," Nate said. "You'll be fine."

Hannah Leigh stepped forward. "Short and sweet. Finish talking before they finish listening. Always works."

"Yes, yes. What's up?" he asked.

"Well, I've learned that once a promise got lost, and I'd...we'd...like to help set it back on its feet."

Clarence blinked, eyes wary. "Is this about that darn *Love Left Behind* stuff? I told your aunt I thought that was bad news."

"I think I know why you've been so determined to keep attention off the dogwood and the board," she said.

He tried to hide his confusion, but the tremor in his jaw gave him away.

Hannah Leigh's heart sank, but Nate touched her arm, giving her strength to continue. "I think you know Margaret Jane is back. She moved into the condos by the dogwood. You might've already known," she continued. "And it's thrown you off balance. You're both acting like you don't see each other, but it's plain as day."

His voice dropped. "She said that?"

"Not my story to tell," Hannah Leigh said. "But I'd love to hear yours."

For a long moment, the room was still. Then Clarence let out a breath that trembled at the edges. "It's been a long time coming. Too long. She was my first love. I never got over her. It near killed me when she left town."

The words filled the quiet like a confession. "I was going to marry that girl," he said.

Hannah Leigh folded her hands and gave the moment the respect it deserved.

Christmas had come to South Hill with more than twinkle lights. It had brought truth, too. The kind that aches a little before it heals. The kind that gives a woman back her peace, a man back his heart, and a town back its story.

She looked over at Nate. His expression was steady, proud, and full of something she didn't dare name yet.

"Let's hear it," she said to the mayor.

And they did.

CHAPTER TWENTY-TWO

Sometimes the answers hide in plain sight.

Nate knew how to brace a sagging beam and rebuild what time had worn thin, but family secrets weren't something you could square with a level or lock into place with a few clean nails. They often buckled from the inside. It was hard to see Uncle Clarence so clearly raw with emotion that wasn't angry, rushed, or retaliating. Today, he seemed a little broken, but nostalgic. Vulnerable.

Hannah Leigh perched in the chair beside Nate.

Uncle Clarence sat behind the desk, hands folded tight enough to turn his knuckles white. The usual sharpness in his eyes had dulled to something weary. For once, he didn't look like the mayor of South Hill, just an old man carrying too many years of regret.

Finally, Nate broke the silence. "Uncle Clarence, there was a letter on the board. We sort of stumbled into who wrote it." He passed the note to him.

Clarence's eyes flicked up. They were tired eyes, rimmed red, but steady. "Margaret Jane wrote this?"

"She didn't tell us everything," Hannah Leigh said. "Just her side. By the time she could get back, you'd married someone else. She assumed you'd never been in love with her."

His brows pulled together, his head slowly moving from

side to side as if he couldn't believe it. "No. That's not how it was." He dropped the letter onto the desk. "I was twenty," he said, the words coming so slow it was as if they were heavier than bricks. "I worshiped the ground my daddy walked on. He was a hard man though, a man who thought he knew what was best for everyone in this town. When he caught wind I was getting serious about Margaret Jane, he laid down the law that he'd never allow it, but I really loved her. I did."

Nate gave him an encouraging nod.

"He said I was going to ruin my life over a girl with nothing but pretty eyes and a smile." His voice cracked, but he pushed on. He shook his head, a humorless chuckle escaping. "Guess that's all it takes sometimes."

He drew a deep breath. "I told him she was the one for me. He wasn't having it, so I asked her to elope, run off to North Carolina, get married quietly, and start fresh. I'd even put a deposit on an apartment above the barbershop on Main, promising her that one day we'd marry under that dogwood, where everyone could see our true love."

Nate had heard stories about his great-uncle's pride and temper. He'd sort of thought of Uncle Clarence the same way. This was the first time he'd ever seen his uncle's heart.

Clarence rubbed a hand over his jaw. "But she never came. That night, I waited at the county line until the sun came up. When I went back, her house was empty. She and her mama were gone." His voice broke. "My daddy gave me hell for pining over her. Said she'd seen sense and saved me from myself. So I tried to believe him."

Nate stepped closer. "Uncle Clarence, why pretend you

didn't recognize her when she came back?"

Clarence's gaze went distant. "Because I did. Even with her hair gray, age hadn't changed her. The minute I saw her at the market it shocked me. I wanted to run right up to her. I still love her. I always have." He snapped his attention to Nate. "Don't get me wrong. Your Aunt Elaine was a good woman, a steady one, but what I felt for Margaret Jane was different." He swallowed. "Like she was the other half of my story."

"What if I told you she didn't want to leave?" Nate asked.

Clarence's shoulders sagged. "I don't even know how to think about that." His voice cracked again. He pressed a hand to his chest because his whole life was built on the knowledge that she left him. "If that wasn't true. How do I ever calm that kind of ache?"

Hannah Leigh's eyes glistened. Nate slid his hand over hers beneath the desk.

"You could start by talking to her." Hannah Leigh's voice carried a quiet calm. "She's here now. Maybe history deserves a do-over."

"Shame doesn't shrink with time," Clarence whispered. "It grows. My father's been gone thirty years, but I still hear his voice telling me that love wasn't practical. Guess I believed him more than I should've."

Nate leaned forward, close enough to see the fine tremor in the man's jaw. "You can't bury love like that, Uncle. The roots always push back up."

For a moment, no one spoke. Then Hannah Leigh's voice broke the silence, soft but sure. "You don't owe the past anything but honesty. Maybe start there."

Clarence gave a tired groan. "Folks think I'm just a grumpy mayor who worries about wreath symmetry." He looked down at his hands. "Truth is, I've been holding a shadow in my chest for so long, I forgot what light feels like, young lady."

"You still have time." Nate gestured toward Hannah Leigh. "Tell Margaret Jane the truth. All of it. Let her know she wasn't the only one waiting."

Clarence's eyes filled again. "You think she'd listen?"

"She moved back to town. I think she's hoping for a second chance, but I didn't talk to her," Nate said. "Just my assumption."

"I think she's been hoping you'd say something first," Hannah Leigh said. "Real love doesn't just vanish. It waits. It can weather so much more than we think."

He nodded slowly, wiping his eyes with the back of his hand. "Then I'll find the right time. Maybe tomorrow. Heaven help me, I'll tell her everything. She's still beautiful."

"Tell her that," Hannah Leigh said. "That's a fine place to start."

Nate glanced at her, wondering if she realized those words carried another weight altogether, one meant for her.

That night, Hannah Leigh stood with him beneath the dogwood. The square was hushed, and the night so quiet it seemed to ring.

"This tree has seen some heartache," Hannah Leigh's voice faded.

"Maybe it's ready for hope again," Nate answered.

They stood shoulder to shoulder, watching the streetlamp

reflect in a halo of light. Bells down at the First Baptist Church tolled in the distance, deep, even, steady as breath.

Hannah Leigh tilted her face toward the sound, eyes shining in the cold light.

Nate's voice came low. "You make it easier to believe in second chances."

Her smile was small but certain. "I was just thinking the same thing about you."

As the bells echoed through South Hill, a hymn of truth and grace drifted through the night. And under that old dogwood, roots buried deep in stories and sorrow, Nate knew they'd begun something larger than themselves. Something that, finally, felt like home.

CHAPTER TWENTY-THREE

The night of the annual tree lighting, the town square had never looked so fine. Nate had spent every Christmas of his life in South Hill, but tonight felt different, like somebody had put a polish on the whole town. Storefronts glowed. Bringleton's chalkboard promised a real steal on *Cocoa by the Tub* for the big night. And Harper's Jewelry had strands of diamonds dripping like icicles inside their window so sparkly you couldn't pass by without noticing.

Folks packed the lawn shoulder to shoulder, the buzz rolling toward the giant Christmas tree like a tide for the big moment.

He dropped the locket off at Harper's Jewelry to get repaired, then went to catch up with Hannah Leigh. He found her near the steps of Town Hall with Aunt Winnie. His heart gave a familiar little leap every time he saw her.

Hannah Leigh's green scarf shone bright against her coat, her hair catching the light cascading over her shoulder. He started toward them, but their voices pulled him up short. Aunt Winnie stood beside her, wrapped in a tartan cape that could've doubled as a Christmas banner. He started toward them, but stopped when he caught the tone of their conversation.

"I just got the call," Hannah Leigh said, breathless, amazed. "I applied for that dream job in Charlotte before I came here, and they want me in Charlotte. In person." She clapped her hands together, barely able to contain her excitement. "It's the position I've dreamed of. Managing corporate events. Not a contract for a single project. A real seat at the table."

Aunt Winnie smiled, kind but guarded. "I'm proud of you, honey. But Charlotte? This place is brighter since you came home. A lot of people would miss you."

The thought landed fast, like a kick to his ribs. *I'd miss her.*

"Aunt Winnie, you knew this was temporary." Hannah Leigh's voice softened. "I've worked hard for a chance like this. I have to see it through."

Winnie said. "Don't let chasing the next big thing make you forget what you've already caught."

Hannah Leigh didn't hesitate. "Right now, nothing matters as much as getting that job."

The words hit Nate like a body check he didn't see coming. He stepped back, letting a cluster of festival-goers drift between them. He didn't want her to see his face.

On the bandstand, the mayor tested the mic. A squeal of feedback nicked the air, then settled. Nate shoved his hands into his coat pockets and walked along the edge of the crowd, trying to make the noise in his head quiet behind the night's good cheer.

He'd warned himself not to get reckless. Whatever this was with Hannah Leigh, spark, flirt, early-stage miracle of a love that might actually last forever…maybe it belonged to December and fairy lights. But when he heard her say, "*nothing* else matters as much", he'd felt the floor shift. Turns out he'd already stepped in deeper than he meant to.

He let the crowd move him closer to where the tree stood ready. He focused on the tall evergreen. Fresh-cut, trucked in from two counties over, strung to the top, ornaments from every corner of town tucked into its boughs. No lights would be lit until the big day. At the very top sat an angel fashioned from lace and tinfoil, a tradition older than most of the folks gathered here tonight.

The crowd's murmur tightened into a hush as the program started.

The mayor said a few words, as he always did, and then turned it over to Hannah Leigh. "Let's bring up our festival lead," the mayor said, voice warming. "Miss Hannah Leigh Parker."

Applause lifted. She passed Nate and squeezed his sleeve. "I'm ready, cross your fingers!"

"You've got this," he said, and felt the truth of it all the way down.

She reached the podium and didn't need to tap the mic. She had them from the second she looked out across the crowd.

"Good evening, South Hill," she said, voice steady.

Everyone cheered. He stared, feeling a little sick.

"When I came home in December, I thought I was just here to help with the festival." A beat. "But this town has a way of reminding you who you are, who we are together."

The square leaned closer. Nate did too.

She kept it simple, talking about the many hands that

pitched in, recipes that showed up on the right porch at the right time, neighbors teaming up for the many contests. "Don't the lampposts look amazing?" She talked about Aunt Winnie's pralines and the town's connection to Minnie Pearl, even singing out a 'How-dee!' in her honor that received a round of applause. When she cited Birdie's "encouragement" of the choir, she got a bigger laugh. Then Hannah Leigh's tone softened, and something in the crowd did, too.

"This year we learned stories don't disappear," she said. "Sometimes they wait for the right person to listen or the right season to tell them."

Nate's gaze slid to the front row. Margaret Jane stood next to Birdie and Winnie, jaw steady, chin tilted up. Uncle Clarence, hard-nosed mayor to everyone else, watched from the side of the stage. For once his bluster was gone. He looked...human.

"And tonight," Hannah Leigh said, "we remember real love doesn't vanish. It might hide. It might be delayed. But it doesn't quit on us."

A sound like a half sigh and half yes, moved through the crowd. Somebody near Nate whispered *amen*.

"Mayor, would you like to come do the honors?" Hannah Leigh asked from the stage.

He lifted his chin, wearing a relaxed smile that Nate had never seen on him. "No, ma'am. I think you should get the honor this year. Please proceed."

"Wow! Okay." Hannah Leigh laid her hand on the brass lever. "Let's start this countdown and light up South Hill and make it the best one yet."

She began the countdown. "10...9..." and the crowd powered over the mic with the rest all the way to a long-winded one, and Hannah Leigh flipped the switch.

The tree came to life in a wash of colorful bulbs as the crowd erupted in cheers, whistles, and applause. Children shrieked with delight. Couples hugged close, but all Nate could hear was the heartbeat in his ears.

His gaze stayed fixed on Hannah Leigh, her face lit by the tree's glow, her eyes wide, her lips parted in a smile so radiant he felt the warmth clear down to his boots. *How can you even consider leaving me?*

He slid a glance toward the mayor and caught something he'd never seen before. Awe. Clarence's attention had locked on Margaret Jane. She didn't look away. For a long breath, they stood in that light, two people who'd finally run out of distance. Nate watched the years fall off his uncle. He stood straighter. Ready. Happy.

He didn't trust himself to look at Hannah Leigh yet. He pushed forward through the crowd, the last of the applause fading into joyful noise.

She turned at his approach.

He braved a simple, "You did good," he said.

"*We* did good," she answered. "This has turned out better than I could've imagined."

"*Is* there a 'we'?" The words came out rough. Honest and unpolished, like a board he hadn't sanded yet.

"What?" Her eyebrows drew together. "Where did that come from?"

"I overheard you with Winnie." He kept his voice low. "Charlotte. The interview. The big move. I just..." He let out a breath. "I needed to know if what's been happening between us is just December."

Her mouth opened, then closed. She looked past him, toward the crowd, toward the tree that everyone was so excited about.

"Were you going to tell me?" He tried to make it a question, not an accusation.

"Yes," she said, too fast. Then, quieter, "Eventually. It's just an interview. I've worked toward this for years. I applied for that job before I even came here."

"I get it." He nodded, fumbled for solid ground. "I thought we were both looking forward to more. Here."

"Oh." Hope flickered across her face, then caution. "You've been amazing, Nate. Our time together has been so great. But I can't build my whole life around something that happened over a couple weeks working on a Christmas festival. This job is what I've always wanted. This is a tremendous opportunity for me."

"Then you should chase it," he said, and wished he didn't sound like a coach giving permission. "It makes sense."

Behind them carolers eased into a round of *Here Comes Santa Claus*. He stepped back, giving her space, giving himself some, too.

"I just wish," he said, almost to himself, "you'd looked at me once tonight the way you looked at that tree, like I was something you'd been waiting for."

She flinched. "Nate—"

"Merry Christmas, Hannah Leigh." The crowd shifted, and Nate moved with it into the steady stream heading away from the stage.

Past the cocoa line and the kids twirling under the strings of lights, Nate made his way to a quiet corner near the gazebo. For a man who avoided drama, his chest sure felt packed with it tonight.

Across the way, Margaret Jane spoke to the mayor. Her face had softened into a warm look of affection. Clarence's posture had changed. He looked way less intense, more approachable. He nodded at whatever she said, and for a second his eyes went bright. Margaret Jane touched his arm, and Nate felt an old ache he hadn't tagged until now: regret.

He understood how it happened. Two people think there's all the time in the world. Then one harsh word, one foolish choice, a stretch of pride, and what should've been easy into a mess.

Don't be them, he told himself. Then he rolled his eyes at the irony; five minutes ago, he'd been ready to sprint for the horizon.

This Christmas wasn't just about lights on a tree. It was about a heart he hadn't known was waiting. The girl he thought he'd let walk away a long time ago, and a future he couldn't wait to unwrap. But it just slipped away.

He didn't have answers. He cut away from the crowd and took the long way home, past Harper's darkened display and the LOVE sign where some teenager tried to dip his girlfriend, failed, and they laughed.

Back at his place, he didn't bother with lamps. He sat in the dark and let the quiet say what he couldn't. The whistle Hannah Leigh had given him lay on the table, silver catching what little light sneaked through the blinds. He picked it up, turned it in his fingers, and set it down again.

"Guess that's the truth about love," he said to an empty room. "It waits until you stop running."

He stared at the ceiling for a long while. *Am I the one running now?* The question sat with him, not pushy, not loud, just there.

Outside, the celebration continued until late. He pulled a blanket off the back of the couch and leaned his head against the cushion, eyes on the shadowed ceiling fan, heart finding a quiet, even beat.

Tonight had made one thing clear. That he wanted a future with Hannah Leigh in it. If Charlotte was a door she had to walk through, he would not be the hinge that squeaked. He'd let her go do the thing she'd spent years reaching for and trust that if they built something, it could stand up to a little distance.

Still, when he closed his eyes, he saw her at the podium, hand on the lever, voice sure. The tree had blazed because she had told it to. The town had answered because it believed her.

He hoped she'd look his way tomorrow with the same certainty.

For now, he sat in the quiet. And for the first time in a long time, he let himself want something he couldn't fix with tools or plans. Something messy, human, and worth the risk.

CHAPTER TWENTY-FOUR

Hannah Leigh woke to the smell of coffee drifting through Aunt Winnie's house, straight up the narrow stairs to the second-floor guest room. The scent felt like comfort and home rolled into one. The lace curtains breathed with soft winter light, and for the first time in a long while, her mind wasn't sprinting toward the next deadline or some bigger, shinier goal.

Peace had found her in the night and settled deep.

Clarity, that was the word.

She lay still for a moment, her palm resting over her heart as last night replayed in slow, sharp frames. The beautiful Christmas tree. Feeling the crowd gasp in delight. But mostly the way Nate had looked at her. Like he'd been waiting his whole life to find her, and then the hurt in his eyes when he realized she was thinking about leaving.

She sat up and pulled Aunt Winnie's old double wedding ring quilt close. The patchwork was soft, even thin in places, worn smooth by decades of love. Her great-grandmother had hand-stitched it for her grandmother and then handed down to Mom. When Mom died, Aunt Winnie took claim, holding it until the day it would pass, like a blessing, to Hannah Leigh on her wedding day.

Hannah Leigh traced the design, remembering how she used to imagine her wedding someday, her own story stitched into those circles.

There'd been a time she thought that would be with Evan. That ended clean, but empty. And now, somehow, she'd gone and broken something new, something real, with Nate.

Was this job worth it? To miss out on something so good for the sake of a title?

Her gaze swept the cozy room, framed cross-stitches, shelves of spiral-bound church cookbooks, an antique brass lamp that turned the morning golden. Everything here whispered peace and belonging. This trip hadn't been a visit at all. It had been her fresh start, whether she'd known it or not.

South Hill was steady where she needed grounding, colorful where her life could use some sparkle, and rooted deep enough to make her want to stay.

She wanted that. She wanted to work here, love here, build something lasting. But then there was that other whisper, the lure of "bigger."

Her mind opened now like a dogwood blossom in spring.

Hannah Leigh Events. "That's it. The answer." She grabbed a pen and paper from the nightstand and started writing the ideas that were flooding forth.

A small studio near the square with white-trimmed windows and a brass bell over the door. She could see it clear as day, weddings at the depot, anniversary parties at the Colonial, church socials with thoughtful touches, a harvest dinner on the green come fall. The new Dogwood Hall needed someone to keep things rolling there. Every December, she'd turn the South Hill Hometown Holiday into something folks couldn't wait for. The Festival of Cheer.

Her grandmother used to say, "You take care where people gather, and they'll feel taken care of long after they go home."

Maybe this was my calling all along.

Hannah Leigh leapt out of bed and tugged her favorite magenta sweater on over her pajama pants to go downstairs. The floor squeaked as she followed the aroma of coffee and the sound of Aunt Winnie humming in the kitchen.

"Morning, honey," Winnie called from the stove. Today's apron was peppermint striped, faded near the hem where a dozen Christmases had brushed against it. "You want your coffee strong enough to stand a spoon in, or you plan to be gentle with yourself today?"

"Gentle," Hannah Leigh leaned in to kiss her aunt's cheek. "And I might need two cups of it."

Winnie filled the holly mug. The same one Hannah Leigh had picked out at an antique shop when she was six. "You look like a woman with the weight of the world sitting square on her shoulders," Winnie said. "Coffee won't fix that."

"I didn't sleep much," Hannah Leigh admitted. "Too many thoughts."

"Mm-hmm." Winnie gave her that look that could cut through a fence post. "Thoughts about Charlotte, or thoughts about a certain Collier boy?"

"Both. Maybe neither. I don't know," Hannah Leigh said, staring into the coffee.

Her aunt took the chair across from her, hands folded.

"You keep thinking your next big thing's out there somewhere, in a city, a title, a paycheck. Honey, sometimes the thing that matters most is right in front of you."

"It's so hard to know what to do."

"Life isn't complicated," said Aunt Winnie. "People make it complicated."

Hannah Leigh smiled faintly. "You're right. I was just saying that about the mayor and Margaret Jane. Sometimes the truth hurts, but it heals too. Guess I should take my own advice."

"Advice is always easier to dole out, then to take." Winnie slid a pan of biscuits from the oven. "Christmas has a way of slowing us down long enough to see what's been good all along," she said. "Gratitude goes a long way. It makes room for what's true, if we let our hearts stay tender."

Hannah Leigh breathed deep. Butter, coffee, grace, it all mixed into something that steadied her. "Maybe that's all we really need," she said. "A little grace, a few twinkle lights, and a warm biscuit."

"Now that's a sermon worth preaching." Winnie brushed a streak of flour from her apron. "Go on and eat before you run yourself ragged. Big day ahead."

Hannah Leigh broke open a biscuit, steam curling up. "You heading over to the festival now?"

"Soon as I pack up these cookies for the church breakfast," Winnie said. "Your mom would've been real proud of you last night, you know."

"I sure hope so," Hannah Leigh whispered. "Because I think I owe someone an apology before I face anyone else."

Winnie arched an eyebrow. "Then don't waste daylight,

honey. Go find your peace."

The streets were quieter that morning, the square soft and still after the night's excitement. A few volunteers were sweeping confetti and stacking empty cocoa cups from last night. The big evergreen was dim in the daylight but beautiful all the same.

Hannah Leigh paused, tucking her hands in her coat pockets. She could still hear Nate's voice. He was still gentle and caring, despite the disappointment.

His words played in her mind. "I wish you'd looked at me once the way you looked at that tree." *How could I have let him doubt he makes me shine more than the brightest Christmas tree?*

She reached into her pocket and brushed her thumb over the small carved dogwood he'd made for her, the one that said *Work your magic.*

That man had a way of seeing right through her armor and into the parts she tried to keep safe.

She drew a deep breath. No more running. No more chasing what didn't fit.

Driving back to Aunt Winnie's house, Hannah Leigh promised herself she would *not* confuse busy with purpose any longer. *I'm done pretending my heart doesn't know where home is.* She knew exactly where she needed to be.

Aunt Winnie's car was gone when Hannah Leigh pulled into the driveway, so she hurried inside to freshen up, her pulse tapping faster than her steps. She'd make things right. Not through grand speeches or teary promises, but through honesty. That's what Nate deserved.

She'd find him at the festival site or at the Colonial Theater, helping the Chamber of Commerce volunteers. Maybe she'd start with, "You were right. I was scared. But you're what makes this place home."

She smiled, the thought warming her from the inside out.

Pausing by the doorway, she glanced back at the quilt draped over the bed, the sunlight catching its rings. That quilt wasn't about weddings or endings. It was about endurance, love that lasts through generations, stitched one small piece at a time.

Maybe her story wasn't falling apart. Maybe it was just beginning.

Hannah Leigh poured the last of her coffee into a travel mug and slipped on her coat. She stepped outside into the crisp morning, the faint sounds of the festival coming to life in the distance.

"Work your magic," she whispered, fingers brushing the carved wooden dogwood in her pocket again.

CHAPTER TWENTY-FIVE

Hannah Leigh eased through the back door of First Baptist's fellowship hall. White cloths, red runners, pine in mason jars turned the long room warm and welcoming. The air carried the comfort of a hundred voices, babies fussing, the clink and rattle of dishes.

Aunt Winnie had given her a mission today. Collect recipes for the church's cookbook fundraiser they'd be working on this year. She had her phone ready to record and a pad for notes tucked in her pocket.

It was called the Christmas Tidings Breakfast, but it was brunch, and it smelled like a holiday miracle. Peppery fried chicken. A glazed ham shining like an apple in the sun. Collards with a whisper of vinegar and salt pork. Buttered corn. The fragrant sage dressing. Sweet potatoes topped with candied pecans. A pot of Brunswick stew that made her close her eyes and give thanks. Deviled eggs in straight rows, dusted with paprika. Baskets of yeast rolls brushed with butter until they glistened like the angel on the town tree.

Hannah Leigh had just reached for a plate when she saw Nate at a table with the historical society ladies. This was her chance. She slid her fingers around the dogwood charm in her pocket. *Don't let me down.* Then, she took a big breath and made a beeline for Nate.

"Excuse me," she said, steady and polite. "Good morning. Nate, could I steal you a minute?"

He looked up. Careful, but kind. He folded his napkin. "Sure. Y'all guard my plate," he told the ladies, and managed a smile that didn't reach his eyes.

They stepped into the hallway, where it was quieter.

"Thanks," she said, wringing her hands, then releasing them. "Sorry to interrupt."

He leaned a shoulder to the wall, arms crossed. "Something wrong? Lights out? Need a ladder?"

"No." She swallowed and tried again. "Yes. Something is wrong. The important thing."

"Oh?" He tipped his head. "You mean that job in Charlotte. I remember you saying that was the most important thing."

The truth of that landed hard. "I'm sorry," she said. "I should've told you about the call. I'd applied before that job before I ever came home. And I'm sorry you heard me say that about 'most important.' That was me being excited about something I never thought would happen. That's who I've been for a long time. Chasing accounts. Climbing the next rung like it would make me happiness."

He didn't move. His eyes did, softening a bit.

"I kept thinking if I proved myself, the rest would follow." She nodded toward the hum of the hall. "This season, this town, you. Nate, you reminded me what home feels like. I don't want to chase anymore when I've already found it."

"Hannah Leigh," he said, quiet, like her name had weight again.

"I think I want to start an event company," she said. The words picked up, sure of themselves now. "Right here in South Hill. I'll travel for some jobs, but this would be home. If you'd want to be part of that. If you'd want to be anchored here with me."

He let out a slow breath that sounded like relief learning how to speak. "You sure? You never looked like the anchoring kind."

"Maybe I hadn't found the right harbor."

He stepped closer. Cedar and sawdust clung to his jacket. "You mean it? You're staying. Or at least I get a say?"

"I'm staying. I love this town," she said, voice plain and true. "And you. I don't want to lose you to a job or anything else."

He didn't answer with words. He lifted his hand, brushed her cheek, and kissed her like a man who now knew where he belonged.

Joy spilled from the fellowship hall. "Time for the Twelve Days of Christmas. Everyone come grab a card so you know what part to sing!" someone called. Aunt Winnie added a joyful, off-key painfully long 'five golden rings' that made the whole church feel better about singing in public.

Hannah Leigh smiled up at him. "Guess it's time."

"Yeah," Nate said, his forehead resting against hers. "Time for everything."

They went back in. Aunt Winnie stood at the serving line, tying on an apron. "Hey, you two. I like seeing those smiles." She patted the pocket, then lifted out a neat stack of recipe cards. "I brought extras. Folks get ornery if you make them wait to copy down a good thing."

"Every time I see you lately, you're wearing a different apron," Nate said.

"Oh yeah. That's my thing." Aunt Winnie brightened, twisting to model the one she was wearing. "This one, my sweet husband Skip gave me. I'll never forget that day. I dropped a pie trying to wave at him through the kitchen window. He thought he was being funny giving me an apron after that, but the joke was on him. I loved that apron. Now I have as many aprons as some folks have socks."

"She's not lying about the aprons," Hannah Leigh said. "Did you really drop a pie out the window?

"Oh, I did. Cherry everywhere. He grabbed a towel and said, 'That's what happens when beauty and grace collide.' The very next day, he brought me this apron. Said it was armor for kitchen disasters." She waggled the recipe cards. "And this pocket is for treasures." She raised her voice loud enough that everyone around could hear. "We're doing a cookbook for the spring fundraiser. I expect your help. You need to get your recipes to Hannah Leigh."

"I'm on it," Hannah Leigh said. "I'm collecting tonight."

She and Nate joined the line. The dessert table came first, as dessert always should. Pecan pies and chocolate chess, a lemon meringue with a crown tall as a Sunday hat, and apple pies glazed to a glassy sheen. A tin of Aunt Winnie's pralines sat near the end. Birdie's ambrosia was as beautiful as a stained glass window with the cherries, coconut, and oranges shining. A card read, "Ambrosia the Way My Mama Made It," and beneath it, "If you know, you know."

"I need that recipe," a woman in a snowflake sweater

said, eyeing the bowl. "My sister claims I don't marinate long enough."

"It's patience," Birdie called from across the table. "And a pinch of salt. Fruit's a diva. Salt keeps her honest."

Hannah Leigh grinned. "I'm collecting for the cookbook. Your ambrosia and Aunt Winnie's pralines are must-haves. We'll tuck twelve recipe cards in the back, then sell the full cookbook to raise money for the choir robes and the youth mission trip."

"I'll print mine pretty," Birdie said, striking a pose with her spoon.

They reached the savory spread. Nate cut a thin slice of ham, then set a piece of fried chicken beside it like the two had always belonged together. Hannah Leigh ladled Brunswick stew, scooped sweet potatoes, and didn't pretend she'd skip the dressing. A deviled egg rode the rim of her plate. When Aunt Winnie gave her the look—the one that said two deviled eggs was just good manners—she added another to her plate.

"Sweet tea?" Nate asked, tipping the pitcher.

"Half and half," Hannah Leigh said.

He whispered, "That's not the South Hill way, but I love you just the same."

He loves me? She took the cup, her heart soaring. They found seats in the middle where the entire room came into view. At the next table, the men talked football and fixed the world in the same breath.

"You line up in a wing-T, and chew up the clock," one declared, fork waving.

"Defense wins championships," another said, nodding at

Nate. "Back me up, Coach."

"Balance wins championships," Nate said, grabbing a roll. "Not too much of anything. Just enough."

"Look at you, Mr. Neutral," Hannah Leigh teased.

"Mr. Starving," he corrected, buttering the roll.

Miss Sandra touched the piano keys, one bright chord that hushed the room.

"We'll sing while you chew," she said. "It's the South Hill way."

They sang "Go Tell It on the Mountain" with the gusto it deserves. People hummed between bites. Kids drifted back to the dessert table and bartered cookies with fierce negotiation. A wide-eyed boy asked Hannah Leigh if pralines were a kind of magic.

"Yes," she said. "The kind you share."

"Write that down," Aunt Winnie said, plucking a card from her pocket and pressing it into Hannah Leigh's hand. "Folks like a story with their instructions."

"Got it," Hannah Leigh said, scribbling.

Three ladies lined up to ask about the sweet potatoes. "Brown sugar and butter," Victoria said, "splash of orange juice, cinnamon, and a touch of vanilla, the paste not the extract."

Pens flew. Birdie pointed her spoon. "And salt? Do you add salt?"

"And a pinch of salt," Victoria repeated. "Automatic."

A blond-haired boy wearing a Santa hat and a grinch shirt leaned in. "Put my mac and cheese in there, too."

"Yours?" His mama gave him a look. "Dylan stirred it. It's my recipe."

"He stirred it," she allowed, and Hannah Leigh wrote, "Game Night Baked Mac stirred by Dylan," and circled it to track him down later.

"Sweet!" Dylan fist-pumped and headed for the dessert table.

The evening unfolded comfortably. They started singing the *12 Days of Christmas* song, and by the last chorus, there were more harmonies than hymnals. A toddler slept across two chairs, sticky with ambrosia and peace.

Hannah Leigh moved table-to-table taking recipe notes and soaking up praise for the festival. Folks asked what she saw for spring, for next year. The answers came without effort.

"I'm opening my own business here," she told Mrs. Kinney from the florist. "Hannah Leigh Events."

"You have the talent to make it a success. I can't wait to partner with you on the flowers. Every event needs flowers."

"Absolutely." Hannah Leigh jotted a quick note to follow-up with Mrs. Kinney after the holiday.

She told Mr. Graham from the hardware store she'd need supplies for a pegboard wall, and was already shopping online for good lighting, and a corner desk. Setting up an office with a view of Main Street felt so right. She promised the choir she'd plan a baked-goods fundraiser with real ribbon awards and judges nobody could fuss about. The plan slipped into place like a dress that needed no alterations—comfortable, flattering, just like it was made for her all along.

Now and then, she felt the pull of Nate's gaze. She'd look up to find him watching with the look of a man whose prayer had come around the corner and sat down at his table. He didn't hover. He poured tea, swapped out trash bags, teased teenagers off the cookie trays, fixed a wobbly table leg with a folded napkin, then promised a proper shim tomorrow.

"Balance," he told the football men again on his way by, and they groaned like he'd betrayed their love of drama.

When the dishes thinned and the choir packed up, Hannah Leigh stepped outside for a breath of cold. Snow gathered along the top of the shrubs.

Forgiveness doesn't always sound like trumpets. Sometimes it lands like snow, sure and soft.

She turned and found Nate on the steps, her scarf folded over his arm like he knew she'd forget.

"You cold?" he asked, tucking it around her.

"Not in a way that needs fixing."

They stood a moment and listened to the quiet. The church bell chimed the hour. Inside, chairs scraped and spoons tapped foil pans. The world kept going. Sweeter, somehow.

"Your aunt's pocket gained ten pounds," Nate said, grinning. "Recipe cards."

"She's gathering stories as much as instructions," Hannah Leigh said. "We'll print a dozen favorites in the back of the book the church is selling right after Christmas, then roll them into the big cookbook for the spring fundraiser. Pralines. Ambrosia. Mac and cheese. Brunswick stew. Those rolls, if the baker will talk."

"Don't forget those sweet potatoes," he said. "When Victoria said the words 'Vanilla paste' it made three women reach for their phones like you'd handed out miracles."

Her joy bubbled up, as clear and bright as church bells on Sunday morning. "I'll wrangle the rest this week. After Christmas, you can be my chief taster."

"I accept," he said.

They went back in and helped close up. She rinsed serving spoons. He folded tables. Aunt Winnie tucked leftovers in containers to take over to the senior center and patted her apron pocket as if balancing a ledger.

When she looked up, she tipped her head toward the door where Clarence and Margaret Jane stood with Birdie and the pastor. Margaret Jane's cheeks were damp. Clarence's jaw had eased. The pastor prayed a quiet blessing over them, then stepped back like a man who knew the tide had turned.

Aunt Winnie exhaled, soft as a lullaby. "It won't be like it never happened," she said. "But it will be lighter now. That's what forgiveness does."

"What are you thinking?" Nate asked as they carried a stack of trays to the kitchen.

"I can see it," Hannah Leigh said. "A storefront with my name on the glass. Binders lined up neat. A big work table. Pegboard with ribbon and twine. In-progress projects clipped just so. By next December, I could be in full swing."

"Tell me your tagline," he said, and there it was again. That way he had of stepping right into her thoughts.

"Gather. Celebrate. Remember."

He nodded. "That'll sell."

"It'll shine," she said, and they both smiled at that. No need to fill the space that followed. The moment held on its own.

They slipped out and walked toward the square, hand in

hand. The church door clicked shut behind them.

"Tomorrow after church," she said, "we'll go by the storefront that's for lease."

"I'll bring a tape measure," he said. "And a pencil I can chew while you dream out loud."

"Bring an extra," she said. "For me."

They crossed under the lights and headed home, and South Hill, bless its heart, held them like it had been waiting to do exactly that.

CHAPTER TWENTY-SIX

Hannah Leigh breathed in the sweetness of South Hill and let it wrap itself around her heart. She had no intention to let this feeling go.

Beside her, Nate tucked his hands in his coat pockets, his smile playful like he knew her thoughts. "You're smiling."

"So are you," she teased.

"Guess we've both got a reason."

And mercy, wasn't that the truth? At the edge of the square, Mayor Collier, usually all business and barking instructions, stood easy among the townsfolk. With his hat tucked under his arm, he nodded as one of the old timers told a sledding tale from '58. He even acted amused when Miss Sandra teased about his "politician's tie," and accepted a praline from Aunt Winnie without pretending he didn't want it.

Hannah Leigh watched the corners of his mouth lift, tentative but true, and her heart eased. Truth had a way of softening the edges the past had sharpened.

"Looks good on him," Nate murmured, pointing to his uncle.

"It does," Hannah Leigh agreed. "Looks like hope."

"Hope is fine," Birdie announced, "but a column in the paper will keep the truth alive."

Hannah Leigh nearly sloshed her cocoa. "A column?"

"Don't act surprised." Birdie fluffed her scarf. "The *South Hill Enterprise* has already given me space. *Birdie's Nest: Gossip with a Purpose.* Starts Monday."

Nate groaned. "Lord help us."

Birdie wagged a finger. "Don't sass me, Collier. If it weren't for my gumption and my southern diplomacy, Margaret Jane might still be silent as a stone. A good story needs a teller, and honey, I was born to tell."

"You definitely were," Aunt Winnie agreed dryly, raising her glass of sweet tea. "And if you behave, I'll even read it."

The group laughed, Birdie bowed like a starlet, and Hannah Leigh thought maybe this town had just gotten itself a new tradition.

"Are you serious about starting that business here, and having a studio for planning sessions and smaller events?" Nate asked, his eyes steady.

"As serious as I've ever been," she said, letting the words stand plain. "South Hill deserves to sparkle all year long. Weddings, socials, grand openings. I'll even plan a party for the big fishing tournament if they want to. Women's meetings. I want to help weave those moments."

"And you'll do it," Nate said, certainty rich in his tone. "Folks will trust you with their happiest days."

Her heart swelled. "Will you be part of it? Not just building shelves or fixing hinges, but part of it all. Part of me?"

His hands found hers, thumbs brushing warmth through her gloves. "Hannah Leigh, I don't just want to be part of your business. I want to be part of your life. For as long as you'll have me."

The air caught, her heart tumbled, and joy rose like the first notes of a carol. She leaned in, kissed him sweet and sure.

Hannah Leigh turned toward Nate, her heart thudding against her ribs like it was keeping time with the rustle of the blossoms overhead. His grin was lopsided, the kind that used to drive her crazy when they were kids, and yet something steadier lived in his eyes now, something she could trust.

"Is that a proposal?" she teased, half laughing, half afraid to hope.

"I'd be happy to get down on a knee for you." Nate's eyes were serious.

She cocked her head, uncertain if he was playing, but then, before she could even make a joke about him ruining his jeans, he knelt.

He took her hand, rough and warm and trembling just enough to make her knees weak.

"Yes, Hannah Leigh." His voice caught a little. "It's a proposal. I don't want another season to pass without knowing we've got forever. You've always been the one I was waiting for, even when I didn't know I was waiting. No one ever compared to you. It can be a long engagement. I know this seems fast, but we've known each other forever. Please say you will."

Tears burned at the corners of her eyes. She reached out, brushing his cheek with her thumb. "For always," she whispered.

Nate pulled a ring out of his pocket.

Her jaw dropped. Surprise and an unexplainable amount of joy ran through her. "You've put some thought into this."

"I have." He reached for her hand.

She placed her hand in his, and he slipped a solitaire onto her finger, and they hadn't even realized people had gathered around them.

Applause erupted, Birdie let out a squeal that could've woken the next county, and Aunt Winnie dabbed her eyes while muttering something about "finally" under her breath.

Hannah Leigh clapped and swept at her tears as Nate stood, pulling her into his arms.

After dinner, Hannah Leigh and Nate strolled down Main Street. A young couple stood before the LOVE sign, hands linked, foreheads touching as someone took pictures. Their joyful mood spilling into the cold air.

"Looks like South Hill's got more than one love story tonight," Nate murmured.

Hannah Leigh leaned into him, warm in his side. "And we're part of it."

"The best part, he said with a squeeze of her hand.

Behind them, the tree twinkled in the distance, and Hannah Leigh knew this town wasn't just holding its history. It was holding her, too.

Two mornings later, folded between the classifieds and the editorials of the *South Hill Enterprise*, folks found a brand-new column.

From Birdie's Nest: Gossip with a Purpose

SOUTH HILL—by Birdie Horn

Well, darlings, what a Christmas we've had! That tree lighting shone brighter than a diamond in Miss Sandra's Sunday hat, and hearts around here are glowing just as warm. Yours truly had a front-row seat to history. And let me say, it's not every day that love stories past and present collide under the same South Hill sky.

Our Hometown Holiday Festival sparkled, Winnie's pralines returned in triumph, and, yes, the rumor is true! People saw romance under the Christmas tree lights. I won't name names (not yet), but if you were in the square, you know who you saw. And if you weren't, well, ask anyone. South Hill keeps its secrets, but not for long.

So, here's my reminder this week: keep your cocoa hot, your ears perked, and your hearts open. Because second chances aren't just for fairy tales. They're for us, too.

Editor's Note: Stay tuned for more stories about the recipes that will appear in the South Hill Keepsake Christmas Cookbook. Don't miss your chance to taste the stories this Birdie can't stop talking about.

As Hannah Leigh read the column later that morning, curled on Aunt Winnie's sofa with Nate's arm snug around her shoulders, she couldn't help but laugh. Birdie had always been the town crier, but now she had an official purpose.

And South Hill, bless its heart, had never sparkled brighter.

CHAPTER TWENTY-SEVEN

The air in South Hill had that clear, bright snap that made breath look like smoke and cheeks as red as apples. Somewhere close, bells chimed the quarter hour. The town felt alive in a way it hadn't in years.

Hannah Leigh hooked her arm through Nate's, matching his easy stride as they joined the slow parade toward the square. She waved to Charlie who was driving Santa in his spit-shined convertible. Kids squealed with their hands in the air as Santa tossed candy canes to the folks along the parade route.

"I could bottle this," she said. "Hope with a hint of cinnamon."

"Careful," Nate teased. "Bringleton's will bottle it and sell it by the tub."

They passed the antiques shop, where Mrs. Weaver's headless mannequins stood like gossiping neighbors in wool cardigans.

Across the street, the Colonial Theater's marquee announced:

CHRISTMAS JOY
ONE NIGHT ONLY

A young couple posed beneath it. Behind them, Aunt

Winnie emerged from the dress shop with a shopping bag on her hip and a scarf flung around her neck and over her shoulder. She'd traded her apron for pearls, but her energy hadn't dimmed.

"Well, look at y'all," she called. "If joy had a marching band, you'd be leading it."

"Evening, Winnie," Nate said. "Headed to the festivities? It's the last day."

"I wouldn't miss it. I don't know that the mayor has ever called for a gathering that wasn't on my agenda." She lowered her voice. "That's a first. And by the way, if Birdie prints that picture of me dancing with that cute little dog, I'll deny it till the Lord himself intervenes." Her eyes softened. "You look settled, honey. That suits you."

"I'm good." Hannah Leigh smiled, her fingers slipping into Nate's.

Bringleton's door swung open, releasing a wave of cocoa and marshmallow steam. The shopkeeper waved them in. "Hot drinks for the walk," he said. "If the mayor called an impromptu town hall at the Christmas festival, it must be important. No telling how long he'll ramble."

He marched over to the counter and handed them each a cup. "On the house for our favorite cookbook taster and her coach."

"Are you buttering us up for Birdie's column?" Nate asked.

"Son, I would never," Bringleton said solemnly, then grinned. "But if you tell Birdie my Christmas cookies changed your life, I won't stop you."

"I hear ya." They stepped back into the crowd, hands

warmed by paper cups. White lights webbed across the square, the giant tree throwing a shimmer that landed on faces like confetti. Folks queued for pictures in front of the LOVE sign, passing phones to strangers who insisted on taking "just one more, for safety."

Near the bandstand, Birdie perched with a pencil behind her ear and her notebook open to a fresh page. "For the record," she said, "Bringleton can keep his tubs. What I want is that recipe for those gingerbread bars you took to the council potluck."

"I got it," Hannah Leigh said. "I'll type it up tonight."

"Bless you." Birdie flipped a page. "Also, the mayor's been practicing his speech in Harper's Jewelry window reflection. That can't be nothing."

Hannah Leigh looked up to see Edna Sue stood in the doorway. "I was hoping to see you two," she called.

Then the mayor stepped to the microphone, paper folded in his hand. The squeak settled after one protest.

"Neighbors," he began, "most of you know I'm a man of few words. Tonight, I've got a few worth saying."

A wave of whispers rippled through the crowd.

"We're a town that tends to what lasts. We fuss over the short term, sure, but it's the long term where we truly live. The dogwood behind me has watched us at our best and our worst. It's shaded proposals, farewells, and first kisses. Thanks to a certain historian and the Collier family, we've found proof that love and duty go way back in South Hill."

He nodded toward Edna Sue. "Tonight, the council affirms what the deed already declared. The dogwood will stand protected as a landmark. We'll add a plaque engraved with the words from the locket and legend. We should plan an annual dogwood remembrance each winter with the theme: *Keep faith through winter.*"

Cheers swept the square. Someone whooped; someone else at their tears without shame. Birdie scribbled like her pencil might catch fire.

Aunt Winnie hollered, "Say it again!"

The mayor smiled and did. "Keep faith through winter."

Hannah Leigh reached for Nate's hand, warmth pooling deep. Not rush, not adrenaline, something steady and becoming familiar. "Walk with me?" she asked.

They strolled past tables selling hand pies and goodies, and an entire display of used Christmas books for just a quarter each to raise money for literacy. She stopped at the *Love Left Behind* board in the market booth on Main Street. Notes fluttered in the breeze filled with regrets, apologies, confessions. A fresh yellow one read:

Sometimes the past leads you home.

She traced the edges. "That one's true," she said, pushing her hair behind her ear.

Nate nodded. "Fits us, too."

Just then, he grinned and pointed. "Oh, that's too good. See her? Deanna Chapman and her little Shih Tzu. Crowd's eating it up."

Hannah Leigh couldn't help but laugh. "Perfect. The mayor might get upstaged."

They watched the white-and-liver-spotted dog prance in a red sweater, a single felt antler drooping over one ear. Standing tall on hind legs, he pawed at the air for treats from Deanna's holiday tin.

"Looks like somebody found his audience," Nate said. "You've met Deanna?"

"Not yet."

He took her hand and led her over. "Deanna, this is Hannah Leigh. She's Winnie's niece."

"So nice to meet you." Deanna's smile was bright. "Can't imagine ever leaving this town. I just love it."

"Sometimes it takes leaving to see what you had," Hannah Leigh said, kneeling to pat the pup. "And who's this dashing reindeer?"

"This is George," Deanna said proudly, feeding him a bone-shaped biscuit. "Don't tell him he's not Rudolph. He ate one of the antlers last year, so this season we're calling him Max from *The Grinch*."

"My favorite," Nate said.

Right on cue, George spotted a golden retriever jingling by and let out a bark big enough for a hound twice his size. Then, with dramatic flair, he launched himself from the curb straight into Deanna's waiting arms. She caught him mid-flight, earning cheers from the crowd.

"His bark's bigger than his bravery," Deanna explained. "He's a tiger, as long as I'm holding him. Put him on the ground, and he'll hide."

The laughter rolled through the square, even over the mayor's mic tap.

"South Hill sure knows how to put on a show," Hannah Leigh said.

"Guess even the dogs have Christmas spirit," Nate replied, hands in pockets, grin easy.

They wandered, the band playing something upbeat.

Birdie elbowed Hannah Leigh. "Need a line for tomorrow's column—something that makes folks smile first, then reach for a tissue."

"Ask Aunt Winnie," Hannah Leigh said.

Birdie pivoted in a wink.

Aunt Winnie, ever ready, lifted her thermos. "Put this down: South Hill doesn't run on cocoa and lights. We run on folks who show up. We run on second chances." She paused, grinning. "But if you want to bring me cocoa, I won't say no."

"Perfect," Birdie said, scribbling.

The choir sang out the words to *Frosty the Snowman*. Children twirled in puffer coats. The LOVE sign blinked for another camera flash. A granddad dabbed his eyes and pretended it was the cold.

Nate turned Hannah Leigh by the fingertips. "You okay?"

"Yeah," she responded with a bit of surprise. "For the first time in a long, I really am."

He smiled. "This feels so good." She leaned into him, their breaths mingling in the crisp night.

Aunt Winnie raised her thermos. "To second chances," she toasted.

"Seconded," Nate called, and voices around them echoed the words.

The lights brightened one final notch. Birdie's pencil danced, cocoa flowed, and George the Shih Tzu strutted proudly in his single antler.

South Hill had come alive again. With lights, love, laughter, this time, it felt like it might just stay that way.

CHAPTER TWENTY-EIGHT

The festival was in the rearview, and the staff at the Chamber of Commerce had shifted from spectacle to cleanup. Paper cutters snapped, tape dispensers zipped, phones trilled under a hum of carols from the little radio in the window. Aunt Winnie's pink clipboard tapped time like a metronome. At the end of the conference table, Hannah Leigh tied red bows on each gift as if she could tuck a good thought right into the knot.

A knock rattled the back door.

"I've got it," Aunt Winnie sang, sweeping it open.

Cold air barreled in, but it was the high-dollar city cologne that grabbed Hannah Leigh's attention. And her senses hadn't lied. Evan Morton stood on the stoop in a fine wool coat, a glossy bakery bag slung from his wrist like an accessory.

"Hannah Leigh," he said, looking right past Aunt Winnie with a practiced smile. "Got a minute?"

Aunt Winnie's eyes flicked from him to Hannah Leigh and back again. "I'll just go check on Project Deviled Egg," Aunt Winnie said, patting her apron pocket like it held classified information. Hannah Leigh caught the grin and knew her aunt wasn't going anywhere far.

Hannah Leigh set down the bow. "What are you doing here?"

"Client meeting at Lake Gaston." He held up the bag like a peace flag. "I brought macarons. Figured your office would only have the cookies with the colored icing on them. You deserve something with a little city flair."

"I like the homemade touches around here," she said. It was the easiest truth in reach. "It's the week before Christmas."

"I'm well aware of that. Couldn't forget it if you wanted to around here, could you?" His gaze skimmed the holiday décor, mismatched mugs, and the clipboard lists taped everywhere. He smiled in a way that said charming and childish at the same time, like he was admiring a kid's fort. "You look good," he added. "Enjoying the season so far?"

"I am," she said, surprised by how simple that felt on her tongue.

"Listen." He lowered his voice. "About D.C. I'm sorry. I handled things badly. I panicked. But a lot's changed. We landed the river redevelopment, and I told the team I know the perfect person to lead the launch. Creative director. Your name's already on the shortlist. A proper title. Real money." He motioned toward the space, eyes narrowing as he took it all in, unimpressed. "This is charming, but you're bigger than this."

The bell over the front door chimed when Nate stepped in with a box of wreath hooks, boots dusted, hair wind-stirred.

He zeroed in on Evan, the bag, and Hannah Leigh in a single exhale. Something in his jaw went still. He set the hooks down as if they weighed more than metal.

Evan kept talking, oblivious. "Come back with me. We'll

put you where you belong."

Hannah Leigh felt the old ache. The one that came from being treated like an asset instead of a person. She opened her mouth, but Nate lifted a hand first, quiet and careful.

"I'll be in the storage room," he said, not quite meeting her eyes.

"Nate—"

He'd already turned down the hall.

Aunt Winnie reappeared with two steaming cups of cocoa and a smile that said she could turn this whole moment into compost with five minutes and a shovel. Birdie hovered behind her like a decorative exclamation point.

Hannah Leigh took a breath and faced the past. "Evan, thank you for considering me for that job. And for the macarons. But I'm not going back."

He blinked, surprise cracking the polish. "You haven't even heard the numbers."

"It isn't about numbers," she said. "It's about trust. Fit. Home."

"We built a life there," he tried again, gentler.

"No, I built a résumé there," she said. "I'm building a life here."

Something in his expression cooled. "This town will box you in."

"This town brought me back to myself."

Silence fell, clean as winter air.

Aunt Winnie pressed a warm cup into Hannah Leigh's hands. "Cocoa?"

Evan smoothed his cuff. "I should go."

"You should," Birdie chirped. "Traffic on 58's a bear

after three." Then, faster than a hummingbird, she snapped a photo. "For my files. I'm with the paper."

Evan nodded toward Hannah Leigh. "Good luck." His gaze flicked over the framed photos of past festivals and handwritten thank-you notes tacked to the corkboard, his mouth twisting like everything was quaint in the worst way. Without another word, he turned and walked out.

The room exhaled.

Aunt Winnie's hand rested warm between Hannah Leigh's shoulders. "You all right, honey?"

"I will be," she said. Then, steadier: "I am."

Birdie tipped the blinds. "Don't dawdle. Nate headed toward the Dogwood Hall."

Hannah Leigh didn't need directions. She set the macarons on the counter, grabbed her coat, and hurried for the door.

"Bring him back," Aunt Winnie called. "I've got a wreath that needs two sets of hands."

"And I want a quote for the *Enterprise*," Birdie added. "Something swoony."

"Birdie," Winnie warned, but she was smiling.

Twilight laid a soft gold on Main. She moved briskly down the sidewalk, pushed purely by adrenaline. She ran the last few yards toward the building. The *Meet Me at the Dogwood* sign made her heart hiccup. Moments she and Nate had spent looking at the letters and notes posted there flooded back. The way his hand first brushed hers, and she that zing raced through her. The one she tried to ignore but couldn't.

Nate stood a few paces off, hands in his pockets, staring at the dogwood, looking like a man arguing with himself and losing politely.

"If you're about to apologize for something you didn't do," Hannah Leigh said as she crossed the grass, "save us both the trouble."

He looked over, steady but guarded. "You don't owe me an explanation."

"I don't." She stopped close enough to see the flecks in his eyes. "But I want to give you one."

He stayed quiet. She could hear the quiet yes within the silence.

"Evan is my past," she said. "I thanked him for the offer and told him no. I chose here." Her fingers found his. "I choose you."

The words opened the space between them like a window in a warm room.

Nate's shoulders eased. "I only heard the part where he asked you to go back."

"Then hear this part, too." She squeezed his hand. "South Hill is home. You're home. I will choose you every single day."

He blew out a breath that sounded like relief braided with hope. "All right, then."

A horse-drawn carriage jingled by on the street, bells tossing in bright agreement. The lights strung along the branches blinked as if they approved.

"Also," she said, tipping her tone toward playful, "Birdie wants a quote for her column."

"Oh, she'll get one," he murmured, tugging her closer. "But she might have to work for it."

Hannah Leigh nuzzled in closer. "Think she'll accept 'no comment'?"

"Not a chance."

His kiss was soft and certain, not a scene-stealer, but clearly a promise intended to be kept. When they separated, the stars showed off as the sky darkened above them.

"Ready to finish bows before Winnie tracks us down with that clipboard?" she asked.

"With pleasure." He threaded their fingers. "Let's go build something that matters."

The little sign by the dogwood shone like it understood: some stories find their way home as they turned to walk back to the office.

Back at the Chamber office, Birdie had moved the macarons to a pedestal plate and labeled them with a card that read,

"Fancy Cookies. May Cause Bad Attitude."

Aunt Winnie stood by a wreath that could've anchored a schooner.

"Good," Winnie said when Hannah Leigh and Nate walked in together. "We've got twelve minutes and a long run of banister." Her gaze flicked between them, satisfied. "And look at that. Y'all are already holding hands. Saves me a speech."

"Don't think we'll be needing any of those, Winnie." Nate reached for the behemoth wreath. "Where do you want it?"

"Top of the stairs," said Aunt Winnie. "And somebody hand me the zip ties before I resort to duct tape and scandalize the Historical Society…again."

He trotted up with the wreath. Hannah Leigh followed, and they worked with the ease they'd been learning. Nate anchoring, Hannah Leigh fanning ribbon, both of them adjusting balance until the whole thing sat right. It felt like practice for something larger: the give and take, the way one person steadied while the other made it pretty; how both roles mattered, equally and always.

From below, Birdie called, "Are we pro-bow or anti-bow on the end cap?"

"Pro-bow," Aunt Winnie and Hannah Leigh said in unison.

"Put that in your column," Winnie added. "*South Hill: Bold on bows, stingy on drama.*"

Birdie made a delighted sound. "Keep talking."

They finished the banister, then moved to the front table, where a pile of clipboards remained to be put in order. Nate straightened them while Hannah Leigh tucked a sprig of cedar under the top clip of each. It was nothing and everything, order and kindness in the same sweep.

Aunt Winnie brought over four plastic champagne flutes filled with sparkling. "Don't get excited. It's just ginger ale, but I feel like we should toast." She distributed them and lifted hers. "To clarity."

"To second chances," Birdie added.

Nate glanced at Hannah Leigh. "To staying," he breathed the words more than spoke them.

She met his eyes over the rim of her flute. "To choosing."

"That's beautiful." Birdie sniffed. "Well, that's my pull-quote." She snapped her fingers. "Oh, one more toast to keeping the city riffraff out of South Hill."

"Amen!" they drank to that.

A knock at the front door made all three of them turn. It was Edna Sue, cheeks pink from the air, velvet hat perfectly centered. "I just got this," she said. "I brought the engraving proof for the plaque that will go below the historical marker." She held out a cardstock mockup. The simple script read:

Keep faith through winter, South Hill.
For All Who Wait.

Aunt Winnie pressed a hand to her heart. "Oh, that'll do."

"It will," Hannah Leigh said, throat tight.

Birdie floated closer like a moth to a porch light. "May I?"

Edna Sue nodded, then looked at Nate and Hannah Leigh together. "I'm glad you two are staying busy."

"We're good at busy," Nate said. "We're getting better at the rest."

Edna Sue smiled. "The rest is where the good happens." She tucked her hands into her muff. "I'll send the approval to the engraver. We'll have it ready by New Year's."

"Thank you," Hannah Leigh said. "For everything."

Edna Sue left, and things were finally as they should be.

Aunt Winnie fanned a stack of recipe cards. "All right, lovebirds. I need two things before I release you to your lives. For tonight, anyway." She snickered and turned to

Nate first. "I need you, sir, to take down the Christmas Tidings Breakfast banner and rehang the welcome banner at Dogwood Hall. Hannah Leigh, I need a final headcount for the library fundraiser cocoa bar event."

"On it," they said, like a team who'd practiced the handoff.

They slid into their coats. At the door, Hannah Leigh paused, touching the frame, the worn paint smooth beneath her fingertips. "Thank you," she said to Aunt Winnie, meaning more than errands.

Her aunt's gaze softened. "You're welcome. Now go do the next right thing and bring me back the story."

"Birdie already called dibs," Nate said.

"Birdie can share," Winnie replied.

"I don't know about that," Nate said. "But if she does, I'd say there's definitely Christmas magic involved.

Out on the sidewalk, the lights winked on one by one until the outline of every building on Main Street was lit. The square breathed, easy and bright. Nate took Hannah Leigh's hand as naturally as if he'd never stopped.

"Just so we're clear," he said, half teasing, wholly earnest. "If some other fella shows up with macarons—"

"I'll thank him kindly and point him to Bringleton's," she interrupted. "We have our own sweet things here."

"Exactly." He kissed her lightly on the cheek. "You're my sweet thing."

They walked toward Dogwood Hall, shoulders touching. Behind them, the little sign by the tree caught the light again like a promise.

Some offers dazzle, but the right one anchors. And

Hannah Leigh felt anchored in all the best ways.

This time, she wasn't planning the moment. She was living it.

CHAPTER TWENTY-NINE

Nate hadn't slept much after the tree lighting, or all the activities of festival weekend, but by Christmas Eve morning the tightness in his chest had finally eased. Some things can't be fixed all at once, only lived through, one good deed at a time.

That afternoon, he and Hannah Leigh walked down Main Street with their arms full of packages. The air crisp and ringing with the jingle of shop bells and the crunch of footsteps on frosted sidewalks.

"Feels like Santa's sleigh," she said, shifting a gold-foiled box full of homemade gifts for special folks in town from Winnie under her arm. "Except we don't have eight tiny reindeer to haul this stuff."

Nate grinned and bumped her shoulder. "But we've got the prettiest elf in three counties, and that's even better if you ask me."

She shot him a teasing look. "You're a flirt."

"I can't help myself when I'm with you."

The sound that escaped her was light, effortless and full of light. "Come on, Romeo. Mrs. Jenkins is next on the list."

At the little white house on Elm, the smell of ham and cloves met them before they could knock. Mrs. Jenkins flung the door open, flour dusting her apron and cheer lighting her face. "Oh, my stars! What have you two got there?"

"It's from the church circle," Hannah Leigh said, handing over the bundle. "Cookies, cider mix, and one of Aunt Winnie's cranberry chutneys."

"Your aunt's chutney could cure the blues." Mrs. Jenkins pressed her hands on top of Hannah Leigh's. "Bless you both. Please thank her for thinking of me."

From porch to porch, door to door, they carried warmth in brown paper and ribbon, each thank-you another flicker of peace settling deep in Nate's chest.

By the time they made their last stop, the sky had deepened to that inky winter blue, and carolers had gathered outside the Colonial Theatre. Their voices rose beneath the glittering marquee:

MERRY CHRISTMAS, SOUTH HILL

Across the square, Nate spotted Margaret Jane stepping carefully down the church steps, her hand looped through Mayor Collier's arm. The man who'd been alone most of Nate's life suddenly looked lighter, like someone remembering joy. Margaret Jane said something, and his uncle bent close, smiling in a way Nate had never seen before.

"That's a surprise—and super-fast," Hannah Leigh murmured, her breath visible in the cold air beside him. "But they make a cute couple."

"I guess when the history's that old, it's not too hard to rekindle from the memories," Nate said with a grin. "Birdie's gonna have a field day with that one."

"She'll probably take credit for it."

"Wouldn't surprise me." He placed a hand on her back

as they climbed the church steps. "Come on, before she writes our headline too."

Inside, candles flickered along the pews. Fresh garland twined among white poinsettias, and the stained glass cast soft colors across the walls. Nate and Hannah Leigh slipped into a row near the back when the pipe organ began to play. A deep tide of sound rose through colored light. The notes rolled slow, and steady, settling the air until it felt like the whole church was breathing with them.

He glanced at Hannah Leigh beside him. The candlelight brushed gold across her face. She looked peaceful, more so than he'd seen her in weeks. He reached for her hand without thinking, fingers brushing hers before lacing them tight. He felt incredibly thankful for her return and this new opportunity.

When the service ended, the congregation spilled into the midnight air. As if Heaven had been waiting for its cue, snow fell, soft, glimmering, and as light as forgiveness.

The square burst with cheers and playful chatter. A child caught flakes on her mitten, holding them up like jewels.

Aunt Winnie threw her arms wide. "Well, if this isn't the good Lord's final decoration, I don't know what is!"

Nate laughed, the sound rising from somewhere deep and settled. He turned to Hannah Leigh, her face tilted to the sky, flakes catching in her hair.

"Looks like South Hill got its Christmas miracle," he murmured.

She met his eyes and smiled. "More than one, if you ask me."

Something in that look told him she wasn't talking about

the weather.

Nate's phone buzzed, the message from his friend blinked across the screen. *Check your email. Think I found your Henry Bell.*

"Hannah Leigh. Come here. Quick."

"What is it?" She read the text and then her mouth dropped wide. "Oh my gosh?"

Nate opened the link, and they both lean in close. The first attachment was Henry Bell's obituary. *Henry Joseph Bell, 84, of Chicago, Illinois, passed peacefully surrounded by family.* A lifetime captured in a few lines. Reporter. Traveler. Brother to Mabel Kensington of Charlotte, North Carolina.

Nate exhaled, leaning back. "You made it to eighty-four, Henry," he murmured. "Guess life gave you a few more stories."

Nate looked back at the email. "Look. My friend says he found his sister Mabel's contact listed in a local directory and left a message explaining who he was and what he'd found in South Hill. He didn't expect to hear back. But the next afternoon, an email appeared in his inbox. The subject line simply read: *About Henry.*

He opened that attachment, and they read it together.

Dear Sir,
Your voice mail caught me off guard, though I suppose I shouldn't be surprised my brother left pieces of himself scattered in the towns he loved. His work was his life.

Henry spoke of South Hill often, and of a young woman named Ruthie. He said she had a laugh that could outshine a church bell and a heart big enough for both of them.

He talked about how she didn't show up that night of the storm when he'd planned to ask her to marry him. From that day forward, work was his whole life.

He carried a newspaper clipping in his wallet until the day he died. A story about a holiday party with a picture of the two of them dancing, along with a receipt for a locket engraved at a jewelry shop there in South Hill. Maybe he hoped someone would find it and understand what it meant.

Ruthie was the only woman who ever had my brother's heart.

Thank you for finding her story. For finishing what he couldn't.

With gratitude,

Mabel Kensington

Hannah Leigh's eyes glistened. "He never stopped loving her."

Nate nodded slowly, his voice soft. "No. He just ran out of time."

They stood there for a moment. Then Hannah Leigh looked up, a small, sure smile tugging at her lips. "I think Ruthie finally gets her ending. At least she knows for sure."

Nate reached for her hand, their fingers brushing. "Maybe Henry does too."

"We need to print all of this out for her and give it to her when we get the locket back," she said. "I wish we could get it to her by Christmas."

"That's probably a long shot, but I'm pretty sure she's going to be grateful to have this no matter when we're able to get it to her," Nate said.

"She's waited so long. I wish they'd never given up."

Nate pulled Hannah Leigh into a hug. *I'll never give up on you.*

Outside, snow drifted across Main Street, settling like a benediction over the town that had held their stories — the old and the new — long enough for love to find its way home.

On Christmas morning, the whole town felt hushed under the snow, as if it were holding its breath in gratitude.

Nate had been up for hours. Sleep wasn't an option, not after the way Hannah Leigh had looked at him last night. He'd slipped out before dawn, let himself into Aunt Winnie's kitchen with her blessing, to surprise Hannah Leigh the only way he knew how, by building something from scratch.

Butter sizzled, coffee brewed, and flour streaked his sleeve. The biscuits weren't perfect, but they were golden and warm. The air smelled rich and welcoming.

Aunt Winnie peeked around the corner, her eyes twinkling. "Lord help me, you look like you wrestled that biscuit dough and lost."

"Not true," he said, grinning. "I won. Barely."

"Uh-huh. I'll let you take the glory." She patted his arm, already bundling into her coat. "I'm off to carol with the ladies over at the assisted living home."

"Hang tight. I'll go start your car and scrape the windows. Get some coffee. It will only take a minute.

"You are a good man. You don't have to fuss over me, just make that girl's morning something worth remembering."

"That's my intent." He gave Winnie a quick hug. "But you first. Thanks for letting me use your kitchen." He didn't give her a half-second to argue, zipping out the door with his jacket in his hand, pulling it on as he ran to her car. It didn't take long, and the defroster was starting to defrost the frost left behind by the scraper when he ran back inside.

He stomped his feet on the mat. "Whew. It'll take your breath away. Thanks again for helping me surprise her."

"I'd do just about anything to see my niece happy, especially with you."

He watched Winnie drive off and then sat at the kitchen table wondering how long Hannah Leigh might sleep. He'd hoped the smell of fresh biscuits would wake her.

When Hannah Leigh padded into the kitchen a few minutes later, wrapped in one of Winnie's shawls, she stopped short.

Someone had set the bistro table in the breakfast nook for

two. A red and green plaid tablecloth, two steaming mugs, a plate of biscuits dripping with butter, and candles flickering in mismatched brass holders.

Nate lifted a mug toward her. "Merry Christmas. Coffee?"

Warmth spread through her chest. "You cooked?"

"Technically, yes. But honestly, Winnie supervised from a safe distance."

"That she allowed you to bake in her kitchen is a Christmas miracle in itself."

"Guess I'm full of surprises, and aunt-approved."

She slid into a chair, still smiling. "I can't believe you went to all this trouble."

He sat across from her. "I wanted our first Christmas morning to feel like something worth remembering."

She tore a biscuit in half, steam curling between them. "You're going to ruin me for cereal."

"That's the plan."

They lingered long after the food cooled, trading stories about past holidays and childhood mischief. The city sheen she wore so easily had melted away, and Nate saw the heart of her, the girl who'd always belonged here, even when she didn't realize it.

After he cleared the dishes, he reached beneath the table and set a small gift bag in front of her. "For you."

She untied the string and unwrapped a leather notebook, *New Chapters* embossed in gold across the cover. Her fingers traced the words. "Nate…"

"I figured you'd know what to do with blank pages," he said, his voice steady, certain. "Fill them with whatever comes next."

He didn't have to put it into words. Hannah Leigh was the next chapter he hadn't known he'd been waiting to write. He was ready to roll up his sleeves and build out not only her dream office, but a future with her in it.

Her smile trembled. "It's perfect."

He exhaled. "Good. I almost went with socks."

Her giggle eased the ache in his chest. She slipped away for a moment and came back with a narrow green box. Inside lay a silver whistle, tarnished from age, but still shining.

"Okay, it's not new," she blurted. "I found it at the antiques shop next to Lundy Layne. The owner said it had belonged to the high school coach here back in the sixties. Apparently, they had a winning team."

"Wait. Coach Rockwell was one of the best coaches around. This belonged to him?"

"It did. I thought maybe it should belong to a coach again."

He lifted it and gave a gentle blow. The simple note rang bright and sure through the quiet kitchen. "It's the best gift I've ever received. Thank you."

They didn't speak after that. They didn't need to. A pleasant quiet filled the space between them.

Later, he asked Hannah Leigh to take a walk. They bundled in coats and scarves and headed outside. The air was crisp, and the snow sparkled, but the best part was the cheerful conversations in the air as kids tried out their new

Santa gifts for the first time.

They wandered, and as usual ended up at the old dogwood tree.

"How do we always end up back here?" she teased.

He shrugged. "Remembering where we had that first spark. It's sort of our place."

"Yeah, I guess it is." She stepped over, smiling, and tugging on his hand when she noticed, beneath its snow-laced branches, sat a new bench, simple and sturdy, carved from polished walnut.

"This is new," she said. "It wasn't here yesterday, was it?"

"Nope."

Hannah Leigh brushed the snow from the brass plate and read the inscription aloud:

**To the stories that waited,
and the hearts that came home.**

Her breath caught. "You made this? Am I that heart?"

"The most special one." Nate nodded. "Seemed right to give the town a new story to tell."

She looked up at him, eyes bright with something that went deeper than gratitude. "And us?"

He slipped an arm around her shoulders, pulling her close. "Pretty sure we're a permanent part of it now."

They stood beneath the dogwood, the same tree that had once held secrets and heartbreak for many others, now crowned with snow and promise.

Hannah Leigh leaned into him. "You know," she said

softly, "I never need to be anywhere else."

Nate pressed a kiss to her hair. "Good," he whispered. "Because I was looking forward to a lifetime of days with you." His chest finally unclenched, ready to meet the day with openness instead of ache.

South Hill stirred awake to another Christmas morning, one filled with faith, joy, and love that didn't need grand gestures to last.

CHAPTER THIRTY

The world had gone still overnight, as if holding its breath after so much delight. This morning, a veil of frost had touched everything in sight.

Hannah Leigh and Nate carried Aunt Winnie's peppermint bark through town, handing out small baggies to neighbors as they walked by. The shops were closed so families could enjoy Christmas together, and Main Street had turned into a playground. Sleds, snowballs, and rosy cheeks, completed a town-wide pause that felt like peace.

Every few steps, someone accepted a bag with a cheerful thank-you.

"Remind me to thank your aunt again," Nate said, shifting the bag. "If I turn into a candy cane from all this bark, it'll be her fault."

"She'll just call you festive and hand you another tin," Hannah Leigh said with a grin. "Resistance is useless."

They passed Bringleton's, where a chalkboard promised one last cocoa flight before closing for the holiday. Mr. Bringleton leaned against the doorway in a red sweater with a leaping reindeer and called, "Tell me you brought that new whistle, Coach!"

Nate patted his coat pocket. "Wouldn't leave home without it." He glanced at Hannah Leigh, with an amused look. "How did he even know about that?"

She shrugged. "He was standing right there when I bought the whistle at the antique shop. Small towns don't keep secrets."

Bringleton tipped his mug toward them. "Now go keep the sledding hill from turning into a traffic jam, and the cocoa is on me."

"Deal." Nate and Hannah Leigh headed toward the hill. Children zoomed past on sleds and saucers, their squeals of delight bright in the cold air. Parents cheered from the sidelines, bundled up with hearts lighter than yesterday.

At the top, Mayor Collier stood beside Margaret Jane, clutching the rope tied to their sled as though it might bite him.

Nate lifted the whistle and gave a short blast. "Alright, team. Littles on the left with parents, big kids on the right. Walk up the middle, no crossing. Helmets if you've got them. Mittens are mandatory. No frostbite on my watch."

The crowd cheered, and the hill found its rhythm. Kids raced, slid, and tumbled into a tangle of giggles and snow.

Hannah Leigh caught herself watching Nate more than the sleds. He wasn't barking orders; he was drawing people together. Every nod, every grin, every hand offered to help someone up again. It all looked like love in motion. She could picture them out here with their children one day.

Margaret Jane and the mayor made their run next, both screaming halfway down and landing in a heap. Birdie was already scribbling notes by the cocoa stand. "Headline," she shouted. "Promises Rekindled in South Hill, literally."

Hannah Leigh shook her head. "She never quits."

"Wouldn't be Birdie if she did," Nate said, his grin wide.

Later, just as the hill quieted, and the sun started its slow descent, a commotion rose near the LOVE sign. Birdie came jogging toward them, breathless. "A proposal down by the sign. Hurry! The ring's gone missing. We need everyone's help."

Nate and Hannah Leigh ran with her. A small crowd circled a young couple kneeling in the snow, the man's hands shaking as he sifted through white powder. The woman laughed and cried all at once.

"Everyone, freeze, right where you are," Nate said calmly. "We don't want to bury the ring deeper."

Children dropped to their knees, sweeping gently with gloved hands. A hush fell, and the only sound was the whisper of mittens brushing snow.

Then a glint caught Hannah Leigh's eye. She crouched, brushed it free, and lifted the ring between her fingers. "Found it," she said, her voice catching.

The crowd erupted in cheers. The young man raced over to get the ring, turned back to his girl, and asked properly this time.

She said yes, and a ripple of relief rolled through the square, up the hill and spilling into every corner of town. Joy spread like warmth, stubborn and unstoppable.

By the time lanterns came on beneath the gazebo, the square shimmered with gratitude. Aunt Winnie waved from the steps, a thermos in each hand. "Hot cider for the heroes."

Birdie announced, "This story's front-page gold."

Nate got two cups of cider, passing the other to Hannah Leigh. "We didn't plan a thing for today," he said, smiling, "but it sure turned into something good, didn't it?"

She nodded, watching the lights glimmer across the snow. "Maybe that's what happens when people stop hurrying. Everything just falls where it belongs."

He looked down at her, his eyes soft. "Like you?"

She smiled, resting her head briefly against his shoulder. "Exactly like me."

"Excuse me, y'all, I was hoping I'd find you." Victoria from Harper's Jewelry stepped between them with cheeks pink from the cold. "I'm so sorry I couldn't get this done quicker with all the Christmas orders, but I wanted you to be able to return it to Ruthie."

"You fixed the locket?"

"Fixed and shiny as new, and we upgraded to an even nicer chain. I'm so glad I tracked y'all down."

"This is amazing." Nate looked at Hannah Leigh. "We've got to take this over to her."

Victoria bounced on her toes. "Oh my gosh, that's great. Tell her we said Merry Christmas. I've got to run. I still have a few Christmas gifts to get out the door before I can celebrate my own."

"Merry Christmas." Hannah Leigh said, then clutched Nate's arm as they watched Victoria head back to the store. "Now that Harper's Jewelry fixed it right, do we have time to go get all those printouts and deliver this to her?"

"Definitely." He grabbed her hand, and they hurried to his truck. "Do you think we need to call first?"

Hannah Leigh waved a hand. "Doesn't matter. I'll crawl

through her window to get this back to her if I have to."

"I promise to spot you and post bail if you get caught," he teased.

It took a bit to print all the documents and get on the road.

"It feels twice as far this time," Hannah Leigh complained.

He reached over and placed his hand on her leg.

When they arrived, the parking lot was full. The place buzzed with activity, unlike their last visit. Hannah Leigh carried the small Harper's Jewelry bag on her wrist. Inside, nestled in tissue, was Ruthie's gold locket, cleaned, mended, and shining like new.

"Feels strange not running deliveries," Nate said. "Like the holiday is almost over. Almost too quiet."

She gave him a flirty wink. "You thrive on chaos. Admit it."

He nodded. "Only when you're part of it. This is going to be my favorite delivery though."

"Mine too." She hugged his arm. "For sure."

They walked inside, moving easily among the crowd until they reached Ruthie's room. The door was closed. Nate tapped lightly.

Ruthie opened it and smiled, surprised. "Well, if it isn't my Christmas angels. Come in."

Hannah Leigh set the parcel in her hands. "We brought something that belongs to you."

Ruthie's breath hitched. "The locket?"

Hannah Leigh nodded. "Harper's Jewelry fixed it. Good as new."

Ruthie untied the ribbon slowly. The tissue parted, and

the gold caught the light, restored and whole again. For a moment she only traced the engraving with her thumb. Then she opened it. Two tiny photographs looked back, she and Henry, young and full of forever.

Her shoulders trembled. "It's so beautiful."

"Can I get the clasp for you?"

"Yes, please."

Nate fastened the clasp behind her neck, the metal warm against her skin.

Ruthie turned toward the mirror, fingertips brushing the locket. "Beautiful," she whispered. "This is a very merry Christmas indeed."

Hannah Leigh stepped over, twisting the locket to the front. "Ruthie there's more." She looked over at Nate, hardly able to contain herself as she handed the large envelope to her. "Ruthie, there are a few documents about Henry in there for you. I think you should have them, but there is one I think you'll want to read first. It's a letter from Henry's sister."

"Mabel?"

"Yes. You knew her?"

"No, but he spoke of her." She reached into the envelope and pulled out the contents.

"There it is. That one," Hannah Leigh directed her. "You might want to sit down."

Ruthie read the letter, cried, lifted it and read it again. "I can't believe this. Thank you both. You don't know how much this means to me."

Hannah Leigh couldn't control her tears. "I'm just so sorry you both spent all those years loving each other and never finding your way back. It's heartbreaking."

"Honey, don't you be sad," Ruthie said. "You have a wonderful man, and you two will have a beautiful love story. And you've brought me more joy than I've known for a long time."

"Yes, we will," Nate said. "And we intend to keep you a part of our lives. We're still going to come and take you to South Hill this spring."

"I can hardly wait," Ruthie said. "I have something for you." She reached into the basket by her chair and pulled out a small crocheted heart of deep red yarn. "A thank-you for fixing something that mattered."

Hannah Leigh accepted it, the yarn soft in her palm. "We just helped it find its way home."

Ruthie smiled through tears. "That's the best kind of fixing."

"We'd love to visit again, if that's alright," Hannah Leigh said.

Tears brightened Ruthie's eyes. "It's been a long time since I had company to look forward to."

"Then count on it," Hannah Leigh said. "Turns out I'll be moving to South Hill, so I'll need some new friends around here."

Outside, sunlight spilled across the town as Nate slipped his hand into hers. "You know, I think Ruthie's right. Maybe this whole town's been mending itself a little at a time."

Hannah Leigh nodded, her heart swelling. "And we got to be part of it."

On Main Street, Birdie waved from the corner, notebook in one hand and cocoa in the other. "Coach. Hannah Leigh.

I'm calling it *Love Finds Its Way Home*."

"She beat us to the headline again," Nate said.

"Make sure she spells Ruthie's name right," Hannah Leigh called back.

"I wouldn't dare do otherwise," Birdie shouted. "Coffee in the morning for quotes?"

"Count on it," Nate said, giving Hannah Leigh's hand a squeeze. "Pretty good Christmas, huh?"

"The best," she said, leaning against him. "Because it wasn't about what we gave, it was about what we got back."

The church bells rang, steady and sure, their notes floating over the square like a promise. Hannah Leigh looked up, the sound settling deep in her heart.

Love always finds its way home, just when you're ready to believe again.

CHAPTER THIRTY-ONE

Morning broke clear and blue, the sort of day that made South Hill look like it had been polished overnight, every rooftop shining, every breath hanging like steam over a coffee pot. The town stirred awake, chimney smoke curling into the crisp air while children tested the sledding hill again and the Colonial's long shadow stretched across the square.

Hannah Leigh tugged on wool socks and met Nate behind the theatre. A narrow path wound toward the small pond locals called *Wishwater*. When the night froze hard enough, the surface turned to glass.

"Ready?" Nate asked, offering his hand.

"As I'll ever be." She slipped hers into his.

Aunt Winnie waited nearby with a crate of skates and her ever-present thermos. Birdie balanced a pencil behind her ear. Margaret Jane and the mayor made their careful way down the path, hand in hand, smiling like teenagers caught skipping Sunday school.

Nate knelt to lace Hannah Leigh's skates. "Tell me if these pinch."

"They don't," she said, with a wiggle of her skate. "I feel...secure."

"Good word." He tied the knot snug.

The ice hummed low as they stepped on. She wobbled

once, then steadied.

"Look at you," he teased. "Natural."

"Do not lie to me, Coach. And don't you dare let go."

"I won't," he promised.

They circled the pond. Children glided past in bright coats, Birdie lasted three feet before deciding to "cover the event from a sturdy perch," and Aunt Winnie poured cocoa while calling out, "Keep your knees bent and look where you're going, not where you've been." Then she winked. "Good rule for life."

They stayed until their cheeks flushed, and breath misted like ribbons of smoke in the frigid air. Somewhere between laps, Hannah Leigh stopped clutching and simply held his hand. Their fingers fit so easily that everything else steadied.

"Do you ever get tired of this?" she asked.

"Never. When it's like this, Winter's just saying 'don't wish me away'. There's beauty right here."

She smiled. "Keep faith through winter."

"Exactly."

By mid-morning, the scrape of blades mingled with bursts of applause. When they finally unlaced and changed back into boots. She felt taller and lighter somehow, as if the pond had left a blessing in her bones.

"A quick stop to drop off skates, and then the Colonial?" Nate suggested.

"What's happening there today?"

He grinned. "Birdie's grand project. Lights, Lore & Leftovers. If you're hungry, you are really going to love this."

Outside the Colonial Theatre the mouthwatering aroma of roasted turkey and cornbread dressing drifted out onto the street. Inside, a buffet stretched across the entire length of the lobby, each container marked with a family's name. Aunt Winnie's pound cake sat in the center with a handwritten sign: *Two slices per customer, be honest.*

Lunch tasted like love passed down. Gretchen Hayes pressed a recipe card into Hannah Leigh's hand. "For your cookbook," she said firmly. "Don't make me write a letter."

"I'll work one up for you. No worries. I appreciate the recipe."

When the lights dimmed, the projector flickered to life. Grainy footage spilled across the screen. What followed was what seemed like decades of parades down Main Street, summer picnics, children waving from front porches. The crowd buzzed with cheerful teasing each time someone recognized someone.

Then came Birdie's promised surprise: a vintage vaudeville clip of a bright-eyed singer who once graced the stage at the Colonial. The audience whooped at the Minnie Pearl sighting. Margaret Jane fanned herself while Birdie scribbled.

More reels followed. Summer County Fair, constructing the LOVE sign, families at football games, even a younger Nate in the background of one frame, grin wide, hair wind-tossed and way longer. Almost a mullet, Hannah Leigh teased him.

Each image stitched the years together until the room glowed with something larger than nostalgia. It was belonging made visible.

When the film ended, the mayor stepped forward without notes. "We all have special gifts," he said. "Stories. Roots. Each other. Let's act like we know it."

He glanced at Margaret Jane, who nodded. "Starting today," she added, "we're forming *Friends of the Dogwood.* We'll care for the square, polish that new plaque, and plan next year's winter gathering. Birdie will run a monthly column for folks to share dogwood memories, or their favorite seasonal recipes to keep us more connected throughout the entire year."

Applause filled the theatre. Aunt Winnie dabbed at her eyes, muttering about dust.

Hannah Leigh leaned into Nate's shoulder, his warmth grounding her.

Nate reached for her hand. "You ready to draw out those plans for your new office?"

She smiled. "Already drawing it."

They stepped out onto the square as the town hummed behind them, full of stories, fun, and faith planted deep enough to last through any winter.

Hannah Leigh looked into Nate's eyes and knew that, for the first time, her future didn't need a destination. It was right here in the heart of South Hill, Virginia, where love, once lost, had finally found its way home.

~*~

Dear Reader,

Thank you for spending a little time in South Hill with me. I hope this story warmed your heart and reminded you that love and hope can show up in the most unexpected ways—sometimes under a dogwood tree, sometimes right where we stand.

If you enjoyed *A South Hill Christmas Keepsake*, I'd be so grateful if you'd take a few moments to leave a short review. Your kind words help other readers discover these stories and keep them shining bright for seasons to come.

And if you'd like to linger a little longer in the glow of the holidays, I've included a special treat—an excerpt from *Christmas Angels*. Set in the beautiful mountains of North Carolina, it's a story of hope, childhood dreams, trust, and the joy of coming home. In the heart of a snowy mountain town, one woman's quest to rebuild her grandparents' lodge becomes a journey of faith, love, and rediscovering where she truly belongs. With the help of one charming contractor, a box of angel figurines, and a town full of Christmas spirit, she just might find that the miracle she's looking for has been waiting for her all along.

From my heart to yours,

Nancy

CHRISTMAS ANGELS EXCERPT

An Antler Creek Novel

CHAPTER ONE

Liz motioned for Dan to follow her to the kitchen island. "Look at this. I'm sure it's my grandparents' old place."

"You haven't been back there in what? Twenty years?" Dan pulled the computer closer and looked at the listing.

"Maybe fifteen-ish."

"Nice. Yeah. Wait. What are you thinking?" Dan lifted his gaze, then cocked his head. "You're not seriously considering—"

"I've been waiting for this my whole life. Angels Rest is practically mine." Excitement forced her words out in a flurry. "So, how do I do this auction thing?"

"You don't." He closed the top of the computer and handed her a barbecue sandwich. "Not without going to see the condition of the house and checking to make sure you're not also buying old liens against the place."

"There's no time. It goes up for auction in the morning. I've read through the FAQ's, it doesn't look that complicated. I need to get a proof of funds letter from my banker before I can bid though."

"You're going to bid on this place sight unseen? I have to advise against it, Liz. That's just plain crazy." Dan ran a hand through his hair. "You're always talking about situations being a 'sign'; well, maybe this is a sign that you should let this crazy idea go once and for all."

"No. It's not a sign to let it go. Finding out the day before Angels Rest goes up for auction is a sign it's meant to be." She scooted closer to him and opened the laptop again. "Look at these. The pictures don't look so bad. Okay, so it's overgrown, but that's cosmetic."

"Pictures can hide a multitude of problems. Very expensive ones, and the fact that there are only three pictures total is a red flag, especially since only one shows the house. The other is an aerial. You have no idea what it looks like inside."

"It's rustic. It's a timber home, what could go wrong?"

"Termites?"

He had a point. "Well, the thing is still standing."

"You have no way of really knowing that without going and taking a professional with you to check it out." Dan leaned against the counter. "Why are you so hell-bent on this idea? You're good at what you do. You have a good life here. Why the heck would you want to move to the mountains?"

"I loved spending time with my grandparents. The mountains are like an old friend to me. The nature. The quiet. I always thought I'd rent rooms out to people and help them enjoy the area just like Gram and Pop. It was a good and pleasing way of life."

"You'd be bored out of your skull up there. No

shopping. Probably no pizza delivery. You do love pizza."

"I can make my own pizza."

He cocked his head.

"I could learn."

"You love your job."

"I wouldn't say I love it. I'm good at it. But I could still do some projects if I get bored. I love that place. It's why I've worked so hard and saved for so long. Every bonus, every raise—I've invested it all for this one dream."

Dan folded his arms. "So that's why I couldn't get you to look at a new house last year?"

"Exactly. I told you. I have everything I need here. I've got money socked away for a new place." She raised her eyebrows.

"The right place. The one that I've had in my heart since as long as I can remember."

"But a person in your position should live in a much nicer house in a much better area of the city. Maybe you'd be happier here if—"

"There's nothing wrong with this house or my neighborhood. Or Angels Rest."

"I didn't say there was. Your house will be an easy sell, but I just didn't think you were really serious about a house in the mountains."

"You never listen to what I say." Which was fine, really. It would be a different story if he were her boyfriend, but their relationship wasn't like that.

"I do listen. Kind of. I guess I just didn't put two and two together."

"Well, call it four and help me, why don't you?" He

handed her a plate with barbecue, slaw, baked beans, and corn bread on it. "Do you know how much work a place like that could take?"

"I can take a leave of absence to do the renovation. It won't be much different from what I do on a daily basis, but instead of opening a mega-retail site I'll be opening an inn. I can do contract work from up there and do both for a while until I build up a clientele."

"You really have thought this through."

"I've been dreaming of it for years, Dan." She walked into the living room with her plate and plopped down on the sofa.

"You just don't get it. My grandparents owned this inn on the mountainside of Antler Creek. What are the odds of me finding this out the night before it goes on sale?"

He sat down in one of the chairs and balanced his plate on his knee. "One in a million, I'm sure."

"Right. Each summer," Liz said, "people came not just to Antler Creek, but to my grandparents' inn for the fishing and fireside cookouts, and every winter they came for the skiing and Christmas festivities. The inn was known for the best Christmas lights around. You could see them from down in the valley. People came from miles around." In her mind she was back there, bundled up and excited as people began to join. "There were carriage rides up the mountain to see the lights up close. Gram would make hot chocolate and her secret-recipe cookies for visitors. I helped. It was magical."

Dan took out his phone and started typing. "And today the population in Antler Creek is eleven hundred twenty-nine, and twenty-five years ago the population was twelve hundred thirty-four."

So there wasn't much growth. That was just year-round population. "A steady population," she reasoned.

"A stagnant one."

"It's not about the population. Or maybe it is. Antler Cree is quaint. It's the perfect place to relax. I loved spending time there."

"That was a long time ago, Liz. And you haven't been back in years. What's that say about it?"

She shut her mouth. That was a fair point. "It broke my heart a little that my grandparents left it behind. I'd always assumed I'd take it over from them."

"What will your guests do with their time when they stay with you?"

"All the things they used to. Enjoy nature. Fly-fishing. Antiquing. Hike to the waterfall. Pop led hikes and fishing excursions nearly every week." Am I really brave enough to do this?

"I guess the waterfall would still be there," he said. "Are you going to take strangers on hikes in the woods? That sounds like a recipe for disaster."

"Why not? And fly-fishing on the stream was amazing in the summer. I used to be quite good at it."

He sighed. "You know I'm not going to wade out in cold water and fish, right?"

She shrugged. This wasn't about the two of them. He knew that too. "You can visit. I promise to have Wi-Fi."

His mouth tugged to the side the way it did when he was disappointed.

"Be happy for me," she said. "Please?"

He sucked in a deep breath. "I'm still not saying this is a good idea, but if you're going to do it be careful. The sale is as-is, where-is, so if you win, you're stuck with it even if it's a hunk of termite-ridden rubbish."

"I hear you. You've made your point, but I'm also stuck with it if it's exactly like I remember, and that would be awesome." She grinned so wide her lashes tickled her cheeks.

"I head to Denver tomorrow night for my cousin's wedding,"

Dan said. "Are you sure I can't talk you into coming with me instead? It'll be a great party and a fun long weekend. Could save you six figures."

She'd declined the invitation weeks ago. "No thanks. I've got things to do around here that I've neglected the past couple of months while I was working in South Carolina." She took in a long deep breath, crossed her fingers, and held them up. "Or I might own a new home." He rolled his eyes and shoved the last bit of barbecue into his mouth. "I'll be back Tuesday. Keep me posted."

The next morning, Liz had met with her banker, submitted her proof of funds, and finished her entries on the auction portal with little time to spare before the auction began.

Like Dan, her banker had given her a speech about buying a property at auction sight unseen. He hadn't seemed any less concerned when she mentioned that she used to spend every summer and winter there as a kid, and that she had a good feeling about this. It might have sounded like an impulse purchase to him, but she'd been wishing, hoping, and planning for this for years. It was surely meant to be. It didn't really matter what his personal thoughts were. This was her decision, and her money, and she had the proof of funds letter in hand. She was set.

Continue reading Christmas Angels in print, digital or audio to continue reading.

<u>ANTLER CREEK NOVELS</u>
Christmas Angels
What Remains True
…more to come.

Praise for Nancy Naigle's Christmas Novels

"This beautiful story will surely put you in a holiday mood. I truly believe this is the best Christmas book I have read this year so far."
— **Susan Dyer**, *Christmas in Chestnut Ridge*

"There was a huge sense of community in this book—a warm-hearted, cozy read that makes you want to move to Chestnut Ridge."
— **BookAddict827 Blog**, *Christmas in Chestnut Ridge*

"Christmas Joy is literally a Hallmark Christmas movie in print… an enjoyable, feel-good seasonal story that leaves you smiling long after the last page."
— **Jen**, *TBR Challenge Blog*, *Christmas Joy*

"A lovely, lively romantic story that is both enchanting and entertaining. Nancy Naigle captures the magic of Christmas and the hope of second chances."
— **Romance Junkies Reviews**, *Christmas Joy*

"A tender, faith-filled story of grace and miracles. *Christmas Angels* reminds us that love always finds its way home."
— **Readers Favorite Review**, *Christmas Angels*

"If you're a sucker for a sweet, clean romance set in a Blue Ridge Mountain town, then this book is for you. Naigle writes Christmas like no one else."
— **Amid Life Wife Blog**, *Christmas in Chestnut Ridge*

ABOUT THE AUTHOR

USA Today bestselling author Nancy Naigle whips up small-town love stories with a whole lot of heart. She began writing while juggling a successful career in finance and life on a seventy-six-acre farm. Now happily retired from a career in the financial industry, this Virginia girl devotes her time to writing, antiquing, and spa days with friends.

Several of Nancy's novels have been adapted for television. You can find the complete list of movies and a free downloadable checklist of all of Nancy's books in series order on her website.

www.nancynaigle.com

ACKNOWLEDGEMENTS

Every story that becomes a book is touched by many hands. My heartfelt thanks to all the people who helped bring this Christmas tale to life.

I was honored to be a featured author at the Buns & Roses Literacy Tea and Auction in Dallas, Texas—an event that raises funds for the Richardson Literacy Center, which provides English as a Second Language (ESL) instruction to help adults improve their lives. It's been my privilege to support their efforts. Last year, I donated an auction item *'Have your pet in a Nancy Naigle novel'*. Sincere thanks to Deanna Chapman for her generous donation—and for sharing her delightful dog, George, the spry Shih Tzu who makes a special appearance in these pages.

A warm thank-you also goes to Sandra Furr Tanner of the South Hill Chamber of Commerce for inviting me to take part in their Hometown Holiday event. It felt like stepping into a Hallmark movie—complete with festive lights, smiling faces, and hometown cheer. Her enthusiasm and love for her community were contagious and inspired much of the spirit woven into this story.

Finally, a huge thank-you to my circle of trusted friends, beta readers, and proofreaders who helped polish this story until it shone. Pam, Marie, Mary, and Sasha, you're each a gift. And to editor Taylor Newport, for her thoughtful attention and final polish. Thank you all for helping bring South Hill to life with such heart and care.

With love and gratitude,
Nancy Naigle